DEAD CALM

EMMA ROSE WATTS

COASTAL PUBLISHING

ISBN-13: 978-1979739443
ISBN-10: 1979739447

Dedication

For my family.

Prologue

LONG ISLAND, NEW YORK

A YEAR EARLIER

Eight years with the task force, and she still got nervous. An early morning mist hung low across the street in front of apartment blocks as the U.S. Marshals and local police prepared to arrest another one of New York's most dangerous criminals. A tall six-story building loomed above them as they rolled out front. Timing was everything. Early mornings, late evenings, it was all about the element of surprise. Within minutes the building was surrounded. After gaining access to the stairwell that led to multiple apartments, they streamed up the stairs like ants. Uniformed, geared up and ready for the unexpected.

Hundreds of hours of training kicked in, along with field experience, all coming together like clockwork.

Skylar Reid banged a fist against the door, her pulse raced at the prospect of death, but never defeat as that was the one thing they were good at — capturing fugitives. Though none of them took an operation for granted, if asked, they would all say it was just another day on the job. So even though the probability of death was high, the need to get this guy off the street outweighed the risk involved. Besides, they had already gone through every deadly scenario that could be encountered. Still, it didn't alleviate the fear.

"U.S. Marshals with a warrant. Open up!"

Again she repeated it, this time banging harder until she requested Scot, their breacher, to step forward. He brought up the steel battering ram and gave the door three large beatings close to the latch. The frame gave way, wood spat in every direction and the door burst open.

It was chaotic and noisy as they flooded in, weapons

trained for the unexpected.

"Let me see your hands. Get on the floor."

A canine barked non-stop as Skylar moved through the large apartment to find a hole in in the drywall that went through to the next apartment. It wasn't a surprise. Fugitives were living on borrowed time. They knew that, but it didn't stop them from attempting every trick in the book. K-9 went in first and she followed strafing her Glock.

Commands were shouted as they cleared each room and took down any and all occupants. She pulled a sheet of paper showing his profile and shoved it in the face of a woman in her late fifties. "Carlos Artego. Where is he?"

"I don't know."

No matter how innocent residents looked, parents would still cover for their kids rather than see them go to jail for violating their parole. Carlos was wanted for assaulting his ex-girlfriend with an AR-15, along with dealing coke.

Skylar spoke in Spanish to another who said they

didn't know English.

Again, they got nothing.

Usually they were on the money when it came to pinning down a fugitive's location. By the time they rolled up, they usually knew the layout like the back of their hand and had often even been inside. As she continued to question, someone shouted.

"On the roof!"

Their eyes in the sky had caught him trying to flee. The eyes of the woman on the ground bounced to the window where a light breeze blew the drapes. Skylar caught it before she looked away. She scowled as she hurried towards the open window and slipped out onto the fire escape. She could hear boots pounding gravel above. Not wasting a second, she hurried up the steps and peered over the lip.

There he was.

Hurrying across the top of the roof, wearing jeans and a white muscle shirt, Carlos ducked under lines of clothing. Skylar vaulted up onto the roof, pulled her

Glock and barreled after the man.

Spying her approaching, Carlos bulldozed his way across the building, only turning for a second to squeeze off a round. She heard the zip of a bullet as it whipped by her. That only pissed her off more. The upside? She now had a reason to fire upon the suspect.

Behind, several other officers joined in the pursuit. That was the beauty of what they did, when they came after anyone, they did it as a team. It was the reason few got away, and if they did, they eventually tracked them down. Skylar burst off the roof, leaping three feet between the apartment building and the next. She landed hard and rolled and was up pounding the roof. Far below the wailing of sirens filled the air. Though it was rare for them to run, as usually her team had the element of surprise, it happened. When it did, she had to admit she got a kick out of it.

There was nowhere to go, eyes in the sky, cruisers on the ground — it was only a matter of minutes before he was going to be spitting grit, and crying about his rights.

The pursuit lasted no more than three minutes until he ran out of buildings to jump to. When Carlos reached the end he peered over, then turned holding the gun to his head.

"You come any closer, I'll do it!"

She slowed into a jog, then a walk, keeping her handgun trained on him while holding a hand out.

"Come on, Carlos. There's not need for that."

"I won't go back."

"Look, you really want to go out this way? What about your mother, huh?"

Four of the other Marshals caught up and again he looked panicked, screaming for them to stay back or he was going to blow his brains out. They fanned out looking for an angle, a way to get at him while at the same time making it harder for him to focus on all of them. He stepped up onto the ledge, and a hard wind blew causing him to almost lose his balance. He was covering his bases, ensuring that if any of them fired at him, he would fall to his death.

"Carlos, listen to me. No one is going to shoot you, okay? Just put the gun down and let's talk."

"Talk? About what? I didn't do it."

"I don't care whether you did it or not, my job is to bring you in. The courts will handle it from there."

"You're not listening, I'm not going back to prison. I would rather be dead."

"I don't think so. You have a kid, right?"

"Yeah."

"Come on, let's just bring this down a notch."

Skylar eyed the other officers and told them to back off. She was breaking protocol but it wouldn't have been the first time. Scot Wilson eyed her, his eyebrow raised, before backing up with the others until they were out of sight.

"See, it's just you and me now. Step off the edge, you're making me nervous."

He cast a glance down while keeping an eye on her.

"It's a long way, Carlos. I mean, have you ever seen the mess that is left behind after someone jumps?"

"What?"

"Oh, I gotta tell yah, it is gnarly. Brain matter, and well… I'm just pleased I'm not going to be the one who'll have to stare at the stain long after you've gone."

"Gone?"

"Yeah, I mean you're gonna jump, right, otherwise what are we doing here?"

He frowned unable to believe what he was hearing.

"You know I was in the middle of making wedding plans before I got the call for this."

She shook her head and took a seat on a large steel air vent while still keeping the Glock trained on him. "Yeah, I'm still trying to determine, should I go with flowers in the middle of the tables or a bowl with a fish in it. I mean, I like flowers. It's pretty traditional, you can't go wrong, right? But the whole fish in a bowl, ah, it's supposed to be all the rage now. What do you think?"

He looked completely dumbfounded and swallowed hard.

"The fish?"

She made a motion with her finger towards him. "That's what my boyfriend said. Must be a guy thing." She shook her head. "Anyway, how about you put the gun down and we discuss what actually happened? Cause I've got this gut feeling. Call it a hunch, but I think you're telling the truth."

His eyes scanned from side to side, sweat trickled off his brow. He nodded. "Yeah. I am."

"So?"

"I want a good lawyer."

"We can arrange that."

"No, I mean, the best that money can buy."

"It's done."

He nodded a little. Slowly but surely, he moved the handgun away from his temple, allowing it to drop to his side. He moved away from the edge. "That's it. See. That wasn't hard, now was it?"

His lips wormed into a smile as she squeezed the trigger and shot him in the thigh.

Carlos buckled, and she raced in kicking the Sig Sauer

he'd dropped out of the way while spinning him over and placing a knee on the back of his shoulder.

"What the hell? You said you weren't going to shoot!"

"You twitched."

"Twitched? I didn't twitch. And if I did, it was nerves."

"My bad."

She got on the radio and called for the others to move in. In a matter of minutes they had him up and in custody and Scot stood there, shaking his head. "You want to tell me how he ended up with a bullet in him?"

"I think it involved me squeezing the trigger."

He eyed her like a frustrated parent and she smiled as she walked by him.

"You know the amount of paperwork this is going to mean?"

"What? He shot at me."

"Before or after we walked away?"

She was about to fire a snappy comeback when her phone rang. She fished into her upper pocket and pulled it out. It was Doug Stevens, one of the other Marshals on team B that was dealing with a raid on the east side. The same team that her boyfriend Alex was on.

"Stevens, I hope you are not going to grill me over a wedding invitation, Alex should have given you one."

"Skylar." He cleared his throat. "It's Alex."

"What about him?"

There was a long pause. "He's dead."

The world as she knew it ceased to exist with those two words. She didn't drop the phone, nor did she crumple to the ground but from that point on, all she heard was snippets. Something about them entering a building, an explosion and six dead and four injured. Scot looked at her, and must have seen the shock on her face. They'd worked together for eight years and been through all manner of situations. Every member on the team knew each other's nuances; they trusted the others with their lives. He stepped forward gripping her by the elbow, more words mixing with those on the phone.

"Skylar!"

Chapter 1

CARRABELLE, FLORIDA
SIX MONTHS LATER

A warm band of sunlight bathed his cheeks as he groaned in agony. Lieutenant Harvey Baker could see it as clear as day. Any second now, he was going to lose his balance and face plant. He'd be spitting grass while they were in fits of laughter. How could he be certain he'd fall? He'd already done it four times over the past thirty minutes.

"And... hold that pose. Breathe in, breathe out. Very good, Mr. Baker."

The annoying, high-pitched, overly enthusiastic voice of Barbara Ratlin jerked his chain nearly as much as her eyesore pink spandex that made her look like Jane Fonda, minus the good looks.

He squinted staring up at the deep blue sky. There

wasn't a cloud in sight. It would be another gorgeous day and his first day back at work after suffering a gunshot wound and being hospitalized. The whole event had rattled his nerves. Twenty-one years on the job, working in the sleepiest part of the Florida Panhandle and he gets shot just as he's considering retirement. The doc told him to take it easy, and by easy he assumed that meant laying back in a recliner on his porch, sipping on a Red Stripe beer, reading a gritty crime novel and watching puffy clouds go by, not trying to hold a half-moon yoga pose at six-thirty in the morning. But no, this was Elizabeth's cockamamie idea.

"Relaxing, you said. Easy, you said. A piece of cake, you said," he muttered as his muscles trembled and threatened to collapse.

"Honey, you're fifty, it's to be expected," she said performing the move like an expert. Elizabeth was a dark-haired beauty, with an athletic figure. They'd been married almost as long as he had to the Franklin County Sheriff's Department. She worked at an antique shop in town.

Sweat dripped off his brow, and it didn't help that their two teenage kids Michael and Payton were standing on the deck tucking into a large bowl of melon. Every few minutes, Michael would tease him by lifting up a piece and then gobbling it up. All he wanted to do was go take a shower, have a hot cup of coffee and get ready for work.

Two weeks of yoga in the morning was starting to make him feel like a pretzel. He ached more now than he had before. As much as he didn't want the additional embarrassment, he decided to let himself collapse.

"Oh, Mr. Baker, and you were so close."

"To death's door? Yeah, I was beginning to see the light," he said getting up and brushing himself off. "Actually it was a bee, it was buzzing around my face," he said, coming up with another excuse.

"Well there is always tomorrow," Barbara said, hopping up and bouncing around like a jack-in-the-box. Elizabeth grinned, she knew he was lying.

"I'm gonna take a shower and get ready."

"Are you sure it's wise to go back? The doctor said a few more weeks, if you want."

"It's all healed up. Besides, I'm getting physical therapy."

She got up and looped her arm around his. "Thanks, Barbara, see you next week."

"You don't want me here tomorrow?"

"I think Harvey here needs a few days off."

"Alright," she said grabbing her bottle of water and slinging a towel over her shoulder as she waltzed off, singing some peppy tune about life being beautiful. As soon as she was out of earshot Elizabeth continued.

"Now you know the doc wasn't referring to the injury," she said touching the area near his left shoulder. "He's worried about your state of mind."

"And I'm worried about his," he said joking as they climbed the wood steps up onto the back porch. "Besides, I've plowed my way through every book in the house, and we need the overtime money I'm not making."

She scoffed. "We're fine for money."

"For now, but the kids will be off to college soon, and…"

"Stop. You're going to get your heart rate up and you remember what the doc said about your stress levels."

He rolled his eyes. "I know, I know."

"Even more reason why you should stay home a few more weeks."

"Weeks?"

"Harvey, how many days off have you taken since you've worked for the department?"

He shrugged, snagging one of his kids' pieces of melon and then winking at Michael. "Plenty."

"A week here or there for vacation, but no sick leave, except four days when you had the flu."

"It's a small department, and criminals don't let up. In fact they are supposed to be hiring someone to help out with the load. So I better get in there before they decide they don't need me."

"But you need to take care of yourself. You're important too, just as much as those residents out there."

He slipped his arm around her waist and brought her in tight. "Important? Well, maybe you can show me how important by joining me upstairs in the shower."

"Harvey," Elizabeth's eyes widened as she tapped his arm playfully. "There's kids."

"Oh, seriously, Dad!" Payton said.

"That's gross," both kids said in unison.

***

Five minutes south of River Road, in the heart of the Moorings of Carrabelle, Skylar's eyes fluttered open to the privacy of the 50-foot catamaran. The drone of the air conditioning masked the early morning activities of the outside world. Though the boat had three cabins, with a double on the left, twins on the right and a double upfront, she'd only slept once on the full-size bed in the stateroom. Since arriving in Florida, she'd seen very little of the town. The dark curtains blocked out the intense sun and the prying eyes of people on neighboring craft.

Several bottles of open rum were on the counter, along with beer. Her clothes were sprawled across the salon or what she preferred to call the living area as that's essentially what it was. She was lying back with nothing on except a pair of panties and bra. Her long black hair draped over her face. The taste of the previous night's beer mixed with the feeling of nausea was becoming all too familiar.

Skylar rolled off the settee bench seat and reached over to catch a glimpse of life that continued to go on. Bright light burned her eyes, and she squinted before reaching for a half-drunk bottle of beer and taking a swig. A quick glance at the time and she contemplated going back to sleep, and repeating the cycle she'd been in for the past six months since losing him, before her superiors stepped in and reeled her in. The words echoed in her mind.

"You can't keep this up. You're a damn fine Marshal. One of our best, and we don't want to lose you but we think it's time, Skylar, you took a break. Take some leave. Figure out what you want. Go stay somewhere sunny, grieve, do whatever it is you need to do to get your head back in the game, then in a month if you still want this, come on back

and we'll reevaluate, or…"

"I'm done."

Before they could even finish she'd tossed her badge and gun down.

She breathed in deeply and placed the beer bottle on the counter, got up and made her way into the washroom. She caught a glimpse of herself in the mirror before taking a shower. Her body was strong, athletic, and she wore scars like badges of honor. Bullet wounds from her days as a cop in New York, long before she became a Marshal.

As she turned on the hot water and it washed over her, she thought about all the decisions she'd made that had led up to this point. Graduating college, serving with the New York Police Department for nine years, before spending another eight with the Marshals. It felt like she was going backwards, losing a part of her identity, but maybe that wasn't her to begin with, just something she told herself.

Losing Alex had rocked her world and unearthed all manner of issues she wasn't aware she had. *Go back to your roots,* her father told her. Maybe there, you'll rediscover who it is you want to be.

***

Harvey slipped into his forest green uniform and once again felt the swell of pride that came from wearing it. He stood in front of the mirror, his hair was all but gone, his skin a deep bronze from weeks of sitting in the sun. Retirement? It seemed foreign to him. He shook his head, it made sense, especially after nearly losing his life. Elizabeth had been harping on at him about how he'd done his time. Twenty years was more than enough. He had nothing left to prove. She was right, even though he had for the longest time had his eye on becoming captain, sheriff even. Now that didn't quite have the appeal it once did. It just meant more police politics, and he'd had his hands full of enough of that on the way up to becoming lieutenant and working as part of the special investigations unit. What would he do if he retired? Play golf? Mow his lawn? Listen to his neighbor, Mrs. Penderwick, moan about everything from the weather to the government? He shuddered at the thought of it. Fifty, he still had some good years left in him. No sir, retirement could wait. Injury or not, he needed to stay busy.

***

Skylar popped the lid on the can of coffee and gazed into the emptiness. Great. She went over to the coffee maker and lifted the lid where she was greeted by the sight of yesterday's used coffee granules. She dumped the small dime-sized remains on top of the rest and closed the lid and went about filling up the reservoir with water. It would taste like crap but it was better than nothing. Money was tight, another reason why she was taking this job. Hell, had it not been for Scot, she would have been still looking for an apartment. He'd had the boat for four years, but hadn't made much use of it lately. It was his baby, a dream he'd always had of owning a catamaran and spending time by the water. But as usual, life got in the way. Being a U.S. Marshal dominated what little time they had in their lives, even more so than when she was a regular cop.

Now it was home, for a small monthly fee. At least until she could find her own place.

She flipped the lid on the pizza box from last night and pulled out a cheese slice. It was cold, and liable to add a few pounds to her ass but she didn't care. It saved shopping, cooking and all of those extras that she'd come to despise. It wasn't always that way.

She leaned against the counter and chewed over what the day would hold. The work would be different, more focus on solving than capturing, and she figured there wouldn't be much to solve in a sleepy county like Franklin. But it would give her a chance to slow down and take things easy. That's what she needed now. The fast lane she'd lived her life in up until now hadn't allowed for that. She smoothed back her hair into a ponytail and went about getting dressed as the coffee maker gurgled. Skylar slid into a pair of blue jeans, a body-hugging green shirt and a waist-length leather jacket. In her last line of work they dressed for comfort.

Uniforms were rare to see, except on the cops who joined them on hunts. She slipped into a pair of flat boots and brought the tight jeans over the top.

After emptying the sludgy-looking coffee into a mug, she added some extra cold water, and a touch of milk and knocked it back in large gulps. Skylar winced and spat it into the sink. Now that was nasty. Yep, it was gonna be a good morning.

***

As Harvey got out of his black SUV behind the one-story, tan stucco building, several deputies waved. "Welcome back, Baker, glad to see you're not wearing spandex."

"What?" He frowned, and they disappeared inside. He adjusted his sunglasses and rolled his shoulder, feeling it ache. *Maybe I should have stayed home a week longer.* Inside, the department was your typical run-of-the-mill office — phones ringing off the hook, deputies punching keys and a resident filing a complaint at the front desk over some land dispute.

Deputies Reznik and Hanson tipped their hats and smirked as if privy to some inside joke. He didn't get along with them at the best of times. Their desperate need to prove themselves overshadowed what common sense they had.

"Good to see you back, Baker," someone yelled.

In the far corner of the room was his desk. He took over his small leather bag with lunch inside and set it down and stared at all the greeting cards and balloons filling up his desk. He turned one, and it had a photoshopped photo of his head attached to the body of some woman from a 1980s-style workout video.

"Very funny!" he said before ripping it off.

News traveled fast and no doubt Barbara had been flapping her gums.

"Hey Baker…"

"Don't even say it," Harvey muttered to Captain Joe Davenport while scowling at the two who he knew were responsible for the photoshopped image. Both of them were stifling laughs.

"Can I get a word with you?" he asked.

"Yeah, sure thing." Harvey leg bumped the table and the screensaver on the computer flicked off to reveal a desktop image of him doing some downward dog pose. Hanson and Reznik were killing themselves with laughter and exchanging some off-the-cuff remarks. Harvey rolled his dark eyes as he headed into the captain's office.

"Two weeks early. You sure you are up to this?"

"Someone obviously thinks I am," he said peering out through the slatted blinds.

"Yeah, I heard about that. You don't strike me as a yoga man."

It wasn't embarrassment he felt, well, maybe just a little. It was frustration. He figured he wouldn't be able to live this one down. The whole department would be riding him on it for a while. Unfortunately there was still an old boys' club mentality. Then again, yoga wasn't exactly the manliest thing to be found doing.

"Anyway, it's good to have you back. Tell Elizabeth I'm much obliged." He walked over and patted his shoulder, causing him to wince.

"Oh shoot, is that the one?"

"That's the one."

Davenport grimaced. "So, anyway, it's perfect timing, I mean you being back and all. You have a new partner who starts today." Davenport turned and handed him a folder. "U.S. Marshal from New York, was a cop for nine years before that. In fact there's very little that she hasn't done. Her track record is out of this world. Sure, she has some baggage but the chances of finding someone with her level of expertise and insights into the criminal mind, are pretty slim nowadays."

"She?"

"Skylar Reid will be working as an investigator. It was either her or a transfer from Collier County and well, the guy would have only had seven years behind him. I thought it would be good to bring in some fresh blood."

"A U.S. Marshal? But they don't even solve crimes."

"I'm not sure they would agree with you on that. Look, just look over her details and get her up to speed on how things work around here. Keep me updated."

Harvey walked out of the office and took a seat at his desk. He'd never worked with anyone before. Of course, he'd worked alongside other deputies but driving around and sharing his airspace with someone he didn't know? A female partner? What was Elizabeth going to make of this?

Reznik jumped up and slammed a phone down.

"Baker, first day back I thought you might like to handle this. It's a nice easy one for you. Seems there is a dispute down at Ray's Convenience."

Chapter 2

Ray's Convenience was a dingy store slash gas station on the corner of St. James Avenue and 5th Street. They sold cheap gas, and god-awful coffee but he had made a name for himself because he gave out free candy to kids, so the parents loved him and well… that was just one of the many ways he managed to lure in unwitting tourists and locals alike.

Disputes in Carrabelle ranged from arguments between spouses through to anything and everything. Folks had been known to argue about two flies crawling up a wall if it meant being right. Harvey took in the sights and sounds of the town as he made his way over. He felt good about this day. First day back and it felt like the right choice. He cast a glance at the folder on his passenger seat. The whole getting a new partner wasn't exactly what he had in mind but once the captain saw they didn't get along, he would soon reassign her to someone else and he could get back to doing what he did best — writing tickets, and contemplating how he would spend his retirement, if and when he decided to call it quits.

Pete Summers, a local mechanic, spotted him as he drove by and tossed up a hand. Harvey gave his usual salute and turned down on to St. James Avenue. He figured the dispute was probably over gas, or some of Ray's false advertising. Like many car dealers in the area, he would put out flyers in the local paper to lure people into the store. It was always the same crap. Two-for-one deals on items that were no longer in stock, or some free item that when people asked about it, required them paying for another product to get it. What most people didn't know was Ray had worked as a salesman for the Chrysler dealership for ten years before he took over the gas station and convenience store. He knew all the tricks of the trade to getting people in the door, and as he would say, 90% of the challenge any business faced was getting folks in the door. Closing a deal, well that was easy when you could look into someone's eyes and make them feel guilty. Yeah, he was a real slime.

The SUV bounced up onto the curb, and he parked at the side of the station. He popped a stick of mint chewing gum in his mouth before pushing out and heading on inside. As he was going in, he noticed two vehicles. — A beat-up truck with more holes in it than Swiss cheese and a ghetto-looking Honda that looked as if it had been tricked out with all the latest customization options that would make folks turn their head.

As he got closer to the door, he could hear arguing.

"You're a liar. It says it right here, I buy one pack, I get the second pack for free."

"That's an advertising error."

"Oh, like the one you printed last week?"

"Look, I told you not to come here anyway, so get out."

Harvey noticed two individuals in the store the moment he walked in. One was a dirty-looking meth head going by the name Cole Watson. He had a rap sheet a mile long, had been in and out of juvenile detention centers and up until recently hadn't been seen in Carrabelle for several months. Behind the counter, Ray was stabbing his finger toward Cole. For someone that ran a convenience store, he dressed as if he was working at the stock exchange on Wall Street. He always had a crisp striped shirt; with a different color tie every day, and a pair of black slacks.

"Calm down," Harvey said. "It's not even eight o'clock."

"At last. Lieutenant, you want to arrest this man, he's been threatening me since he walked in here."

"Threatening? You are unbelievable." Cole held up one of the colorful flyers and stabbed it with his bony finger. "Right there, read it for yourself. There has to be a law against this. That's straight-up fraud."

"You need to read the fine print on the back, it states quite clearly that—"

"Oh screw you and your fine print."

Harvey took the flyer from him and had a glance at it. "You have to admit, Ray, that's kind of pushing the line."

"So you're taking his side?" Ray asked.

"I'm not taking anyone's side. I'm trying to get both of you to calm down."

Right then out the corner of his eye, he noticed movement in the mirror that was positioned in the top corner of the room. He could see someone wearing a hoodie standing by the refrigerator at the back of the store.

"Friend of yours?" Harvey asked, making a nudge with his head to the mirror and looking back at Cole.

"No. I'm here alone. Look, what are you going to do about this? This fool owes me a pack of smokes and I'm not leaving until I get them."

"The fine print states—"

"To hell with your fine print. You say that one more time and I'm climbing over that counter and I'll—"

Harvey put out his hand. "That's enough. Just settle down and maybe we can get this figured out."

"The only way this is getting figured out is when I'm walking out of this store with two packs of smokes and five bucks off my gas. Which is another thing, I might add. This fool advertises he has the cheapest gas in town, and then when I take him up on it, he says I need some Ray Bucks to be able to get the five bucks off!" He snatched the paper out of Harvey's hand and tossed it front of Ray. "Look, read it yourself. It's printed in bold pretty damn clear. Five bucks of gas when you spend more than thirty bucks. I filled my car with thirty, so this should cost me twenty-five but you want to charge me thirty. That's false advertising."

"No, you get a five-dollar coupon after thirty bucks, and that can be used towards your next purchase. You need to read the fine print."

Cole lunged forward towards the counter and Harvey had just about enough of this. He stepped in and grabbed a hold of the back of Cole's collar yanking him back. Cole wheeled around and blindsided him with a hook under the chin that sent him crashing into a display of birthday cards.

"Now look at what you made me do!" he shouted at Ray before reaching around and pulling a handgun from the back of his waistband and raking it back and forth between Ray and Harvey. "All I wanted was the goddamn cigarettes."

Harvey groaned feeling pain shoot through his pelvis. "Cole, you don't want to do this. Just put the gun down, and we'll get this settled."

"Settled? You mean tossing me in the back of your SUV and taking me down to the station. I don't think so. Been there, done that. I know how that plays out. No, I want the cigarettes, the five dollars off and then I'm outta here." He turned his attention back to Ray and waved the gun in his face. "Come on! What are you waiting for? Get it for me now. And while you're at it, you can give me what you have in the cash register, just for being a jerk."

"Okay, okay!"

Harvey inched his hand towards his piece which was under his jacket when Cole noticed.

"What the hell do you think you're doing?"

Harvey threw up his hands. The last thing he wanted was a bullet in him and this kid was capable of it. He'd already been charged with reckless driving and possession of a firearm without a license. How the hell he managed to get out of jail was just another reason why Harvey was considering retirement. The world of being a police officer was a hell of a lot different to the way it was back when he first got started.

Cole reached down and grabbed Harvey's piece while pressing the cold barrel of his own gun to the front of Harvey's head. "Still want to be the hero or do I need to put a bullet in you?"

"No, I'm good."

Right then there was a clatter of bottles, and one sounded like it smashed.

A female voice came from the back of the store. "Ah, geez Louise. Seriously?"

Cole frowned, looked at Ray, then back at Harvey. "Hey lady, get your ass out here."

There was a tense few minutes as they waited for her to emerge. Instead of coming to the front, she continued to make a ruckus. Glass clinked, then came a hiss of what sounded like a can being opened. That was followed by slurping. "Now that's what I'm talking about."

Cole was bouncing on the balls of his feet, his eyes darting back and forth. Everyone was trying to make sense of what was going on. Harvey was looking for his moment to pounce. Cole shifted into the aisle.

"You!"

"Who me?" the voice replied.

"Yeah, get up here now."

Boots pounded against the floor and then a figure emerged at the end holding a basket full of alcohol. "Oh, and I need a packet of those," she said reaching for a box of feminine hygiene products. She plunked all the goods down on the counter completely ignoring the fact that Cole was holding a gun to the back of her head.

"Get on the floor," Cole ordered.

The hooded woman didn't even flinch. "Hey look, I

dropped a bottle of rum back there, it's a real mess. Sorry but the darn thing slipped out of my hands. Oh, and I opened a can of beer. I was real thirsty. What do I owe you?"

Ray was standing behind the counter with the cash register drawer open and his hands up in the air.

"Did you not hear me?"

That's when Harvey got his first look at the woman. She turned around and dropped her hood. She was in her late thirties, long dark hair, and pretty eyes. She was around five foot three and had an hourglass figure.

"Oh hey, is that the P226 or the P320 Sig Sauer? I always get them mixed up." She turned and made a comment to Ray about how she'd always preferred the 229.

"What?" Cole asked, slightly caught off-guard.

"The gun."

"It's a P226," he said, his eyes bouncing back to Harvey who was thinking that his chances of being able to get up without Cole shooting her or him were slim to none. He couldn't even reach his radio.

"Look, I don't mean to be nosy as I'm still new to the town, and all, but..." she thumbed over her shoulder. "Wouldn't you do better holding up the Centennial Bank? I mean, a pack of smokes, and a hundred and sixty bucks in cash isn't exactly big stakes, now is it?"

"There's actually three hundred and sixteen in the till, give or take a few cents."

"Shut the hell up!" Cole shouted.

"Look, man, are you going to shoot or what? I really have a busy day ahead of me, and this is kind of holding me up." She let out a chuckle. "No pun intended."

Harvey's eyed widened. What the hell was she saying? He thought Cole was crazy, but this lady was on a whole other level.

"Well, I haven't decided what I'm gonna do. Right now, I just need my smokes and the cash."

"Okay, well let's get you that." She clicked her fingers. "Ray, the smokes, the cash, let's speed this thing up. I don't have all day and I don't think our friend here does either." She glanced at her watch. "I'm figuring the cops will be here soon and under the circumstances, and first impressions and all, this might not be the best situation to show my A-side."

"Would you shut up!" Cole said, pushing the gun into her forehead.

She continued. "You know, forget the beer, Ray, I'll come back later and get it."

"Don't move!" Cole bellowed.

"Okay! I was really hoping to avoid this but…"

As she turned, she reacted in a split second. It happened so fast, Harvey didn't even catch what she did. One second Cole was holding a gun to her face, the next it was on the floor and he was crying out in pain. But that was only half of it, she stepped in bringing him down to the ground and twisting around until she had his arm in a lock.

Harvey scrambled to his feet, brought out a pair of cuffs and slapped them on him and took over from there.

"What the hell was that?"

She got back to her feet and brushed herself off. "Krav Maga, and eight years of jujitsu. By the way you might want to have the medics check his finger out, it's broken."

With that said she went up to the counter and tossed down a few bills, paid for her stuff and went to walk out the door as if nothing had happened.

"Hey, hey, hold up. What's your name?"

She cast a glance over her shoulder. "Skylar Reid, and you are?"

His brow knit together in disbelief. "Your partner."

Her eyes widened, and a smile danced on her lips.

"Well, isn't that something?"

Chapter 3

Harvey paced back and forth inside the office of Captain Davenport. "She broke the man's finger, Cap. Now, I'm telling you, she's out of her mind. I want a new partner."

"She single-handedly took down Cole Watson."

"Yeah, and nearly got me killed in the process, never mind poor old Ray. When the meds wheeled him into the back of the van, the guy looked as if he was about to have a heart attack."

"You're missing the point, Harvey."

"Then enlighten me."

"You told me six months ago that you were thinking of retiring, and Elizabeth has been harping on at me about making sure I don't throw you into too many life-threatening situations and now you have someone who can protect your ass, you want a new partner?"

"I didn't even ask for a partner. I'm a lone wolf. I work

alone."

"Lone wolf," Davenport said before chuckling.

"And I don't need anyone protecting me. I can protect myself."

"Sounded like you got your ass whopped."

"He caught me off-guard. It was a dispute. I figured I'd be turfing him out and that would be the end of that. How did I know he would have a gun on him?"

"His history."

"Okay now you're making me sound like a fool."

Davenport leaned back in his chair. "Harvey, take a seat."

"I don't want to sit," he replied.

"It wasn't a question. Now sit. You're sending my blood pressure through the roof."

Harvey slumped down and looked at the watch on his arm.

"You got somewhere to be?"

"I take meds at a certain time. Doctor's orders."

Davenport leaned forward clasping his hands together.

"Listen, take her out, show her around and keep an eye on her. If a month from now, you don't think she fits the bill, I'll relook at it and maybe we'll get the kid in from Collier County."

"You promise?"

He screwed his face up and waved him off.

"Get out of my office." Davenport shook his head and went back to looking at his computer.

***

Outside in the main office Hanson and Reznik were laughing up a storm, chatting with Skylar. She was perched on the edge of Hanson's desk recounting tales from her time in the U.S. Marshals. As he closed the door, Reznik glanced his way and then muttered something into Skylar's ear and they all started laughing again. He threaded around desks until he found his chair and plopped himself down in front of the computer. He planned on going through some of the recent reports that had miraculously appeared on his desk. The crimes he dealt with on a day-to-day basis ranged from burglaries, fraud, cybercrimes, and theft to arson, hate crimes, abuse, sexual assault and drugs, all the way through to homicide. It was a mixed bag and no two cases were ever the same. It certainly kept his job interesting.

He lifted his eyes and saw Skylar wave to the odd couple before heading his way. He tried to make himself look busy. He got this straitlaced look on his face and squinted at the computer screen.

She parked herself on the corner of his desk and flicked the bobblehead of Babe Ruth, his head rocked back and forth. "You should get some glasses."

"What?" He acted like he didn't even notice her.

"Squinting. When did you last get your eyes checked?"

"When was the last time you didn't break someone's finger?"

She laughed and slipped off his desk, grabbed a chair and pulled it around before taking a seat. She reached over and grabbed one of the folders from the stack. "So let's take a look-see at what you guys get up to here."

"Hey, don't mix those up, I need to keep them in

order."

"Don't tell me you have OCD, do you?"

"No, but even if I did, would it matter? Cause I can find someone else."

She sucked air between her lips and looked back at the file without providing an answer. The fact was he liked to run a tight ship. Clutter drove him mad, he actually got a physical reaction to anything that was out of place. Elizabeth had got used to it and according to her he'd got a lot better over the years but that was at home. Work was another thing entirely.

She was just about to make another comment when Hanson hurried past his desk.

"Seems we got a body on our hands."

"What?"

"I just got a call from a mother reporting a white male, down in Otter Creek Swamp." He paused for a second. "Looks like the head's missing."

***

Outside the station, Skylar made a gesture towards her

beat-up truck. It was the same one he'd seen parked outside Ray's store. It was a total piece of crap.

"That yours?"

"Ain't she a beauty?"

Harvey stood there looking dumbfounded. "Did you get life insurance with it?"

She put a hand on her hip and shot him a glance.

"Look, we'll take mine. I can't be seen driving up in that. I have a reputation to uphold."

He started heading towards his brand-new black SUV. He'd purchased it outright as he didn't want to be messing around with lease or financing deals with retirement on the horizon.

Skylar shrugged and followed him. "I'll drive."

"Like hell you will," he said, squinting into the sun as he donned his aviator glasses. He hopped in the driver's side and eyed her as she slipped onto the passenger seat, bounced a little and cast a glance around.

"Not bad. Not bad at all. That's some rich leather you got there, Baker."

"Top of the line," he muttered jamming his key in the ignition and starting the engine. It growled to life. Symphony music blared out of the speakers and he turned down the volume.

"Ah, I would have never taken you for a Beethoven man," Skylar said bringing the window down. He brought the window back up again and then turned the air conditioning on. She smirked and opened the glove compartment as he veered south on FL-65. He planned on taking the scenic route, as the guy was already dead, an officer was on scene so there was no rush.

No sooner had he started heading south when she twisted the dial on the radio to some country station and then brought the window down again. Without saying a word he brought the window up and changed the station back.

"Let's make a few things clear here. I don't know how things rolled out in New York but down here, we handle matters in a different way."

She got a wry smile on her face and slipped the

sunglasses on her head down.

"So no country?"

"Nope."

"Ever?"

"Nope."

"Man, that's gotta suck. How do you put up with that stuff? It would drive me nuts."

He glanced at her like she was blaspheming.

"It keeps me calm."

"Oh I thought your driving would do that. You know you are going below the speed limit? We're the cops, you can put your foot down. Where's the siren in this thing?"

She leaned over and started fiddling around with different dials until he shooed her hand away like an annoying fly.

"There is no siren."

"No siren?"

"I haven't got it fitted yet. Not sure I will. Haven't decided if I'm going to keep using the department's or this."

She scoffed. "Yeah, well you might wanna get on that. People around here need to know who's who."

"Who's who?"

"Who?" she replied with a smirk.

He shook his head getting annoyed with her mind games.

"Anyway, I have a few rules. If you are going to ride with me there is to be no putting your feet up on the dashboard. No touching the windows with your greasy mitts. If it rains…" he leaned across while trying to keep his eyes on the road, dropped the glove compartment door and pulled out some extra disposable shoe covers that he'd nabbed from the crime scene team, "you'll put these on *before* you get in." He emphasized "before" to make it crystal-clear.

She started laughing. "Okay, and let me guess, if I get soaked, you want me to sit in the back?"

He narrowed his eyes, and she shook her head.

"Is everything a joke to you?"

"You always this uptight?" she asked.

He slammed the glove compartment door and eyed her out the corner of his eye. This was going to be a long day.

It was a straight shot down US-98, then north on US-319. It took about thirteen minutes if the traffic was good. US-98 took them along what was referred to as the Forgotten Coast — a beautiful strait of sand, oyster shells and boulders to his right and mangroves, scrub brush and pine to his left. It was a real slice of heaven, tucked away in the south corner of Franklin County. As they headed for 319, Skylar stared out at the odd palm tree and old stilt homes built close to the water's edge. The only thing that separated them from the beach was the main stretch of road. Most of the clapboard homes were built ten feet aboveground, in case of a storm surge.

She kept sniffing like a dog and screwing up her nose. The area was known for the distinct and perpetual smell of low tide. Harvey had never really thought about it. He'd known nothing but Florida life.

"Wow, that smell is going to take some getting used

to," she said. "In the city, all you smell is gas, bad Chinese food and piss." She let out a chuckle as if expecting him to join in. He didn't. Instead, he grimaced at the thought. Cities had never been his thing. He couldn't stand the congestion, the noise or the way people ignored each other until it suited them. Nope, Franklin County was nothing like that. Here, the people were good folk. It was a slower pace of living but that suited him just fine. He liked knowing his neighbors, seeing familiar faces in and around Carrabelle and…

Before he could finish the thought, Skylar bellowed, "STOP!"

Her voice was so loud, he nearly crashed the SUV. Harvey swerved a little and then got control of the vehicle. As he turned to see what the issue was, he found her laughing. "Oh Scot, that's hilarious."

She was on the phone.

He took a moment to pull over to the hard shoulder so he could catch his breath. He put two fingers on his wrist to check his pulse and breathed steadily to get his heart rate to slow.

"Right, I will do. Yeah, gotta get back to work. Yeah, speak soon."

She ended the call and chuckled away to herself until she noticed he was staring at her and had turned in his seat. The SUV idled, just purring away gently.

"The next time you decide to yell stop, would you mind giving me a heads-up?"

She nodded, her eyes slightly wide. "Sure. Sure thing."

***

Skylar couldn't figure out what was the deal with this guy. He seemed wound up like a jack-in-the-box, just waiting to explode. She'd worked with all types in her time as a cop in New York, and well, even on the task force they had a few that were a little on edge but he brought a whole new meaning to the word uptight.

About ten minutes into the journey, they saw a brown sign for Tate's Hell State Forest. Harvey eased off the gas and veered to the left onto a gravel and sand road full of nothing but dwarf cypress and brush.

"Tate's Hell? Where do they come up with these names?" she muttered.

"Well you have Hell's Kitchen, that's not much better," he said as if it was some kind of pissing match between his beloved Florida and where she'd just come from. Yeah, this was going to take some getting used to, she thought. "If you'd like to know, it actually got its name after a local farmer called Cebe Tate."

"Yeah? What was he, a mass murderer?"

Gravel crunched beneath the tires as they made their way down a long winding road.

"Actually his livestock kept being attacked by a panther. So rumor has it, he headed into the forest with his shotgun and hunting dogs to put an end to it. Anyway to cut a long story short, he became lost for seven days, he was eaten alive by mosquitoes and nearly died from dehydration. The only way he survived was to drink the muddy swamp water."

"I bet that was tasty," she joked.

Clearly humor wasn't his thing as he cleared his throat

and continued. "When he emerged from the underbrush, they could barely get a word out of him. All he could tell them was his name and that he'd been through hell. Then he dropped down dead."

He sniffed hard and took a sip of his coffee.

Skylar stared as him as he adjusted his grip on the steering wheel.

"That's it? He died?"

"Yep."

She turned back to looking out the window. "Well, let's hope we don't get lost out here."

"This must be quite foreign to you. A number of people use the trails, though. This place is popular with hunters, and folks who like to camp. You ever done any hunting?"

"Nope. You?"

"No."

"You always lived in the big city?"

"Pretty much. I grew up on Long Island. You ever been to the Big Apple?"

"No. All those people. I would feel as though someone was suffocating me."

"Actually it's pretty nice. There is something about living and working in the city. The whole place feels alive, like a mosquito-infested swamp, without the muddy waters, alligators and whatnot…" she trailed off. Skylar was pretty sure she caught him smile but then again that might have just been a nervous twitch.

They drove over a low bridge and she glanced at the still waters covered in lily pads.

"So why didn't you stay?" he asked. She caught something in his tone that led her to believe that he wished she had stayed.

"I…"

Before she could finish, a couple of black-and-whites came into view, along with yellow police tape cordoning off the area. They were parked in a clearing by an expansive swamp full of cypress knees, a jagged display of dark black and gray stumps that peeked above the murky waters like the outstretched gnarled fingers of the dead.

Baker brought the SUV to a stop a few feet back from the other cruisers. Before he got out, he twisted in his seat.

"You ever been called out to a scene like this?"

"A dead body? Of course." Her expression twisted between a frown and a smile. What picture of her did he have in his mind? She was beginning to think he thought she was wet behind the ears.

"Just checking."

He pushed out of the vehicle and took with him his Styrofoam cup of coffee that had to have gone cold. One of the officers approached, his hand resting on his firearm.

"Ain't this just a pretty place to die," Baker said. "What have we got, Miles?"

The officer cut her a glance as she made her way around. The ground felt alive, like she was standing on a sponge. She fell in step with Baker and Officer Miles from the Carrabelle Police Department.

"The kid is over there. Ricky Jennings. He's quite shaken up by it all. We're still waiting on the M.E." He looked past them. "He's not with you?"

Skylar looked over her shoulder and followed his gaze.

"Does it look like it?" Baker replied, taking out some latex gloves and snapping them on. "I hope you haven't messed up my crime scene."

"No."

"You touch anything?"

"Well, we pulled the body in but we haven't touched him beyond that."

"So we know it's a male."

"Yeah. My guess and remember I'm going by the appearance of a swollen body — he's got to be in his early fifties."

"How so?"

"Gray hair on the chest. Like I said, it's just my guess."

Baker walked over and crouched down and lifted up a plastic cover that had been placed over his body.

"No head, so I'm assuming a gator. Though we have a locked truck over there. I can't find the keys. There also appears to be a suicide note left on the seat."

Baker lifted his eyes. "You touch it?"

"No, it was partially open. Like I said, I haven't touched anything. We didn't even searched the vehicle yet. Just a routine look through the windows. The doors are locked and you can just make out the note on the seat."

"How about running the plates?"

"Was just about to do that."

Skylar stood back and observed and listened, letting Baker take charge. She already felt as if she was stepping on his toes just by being there.

"I know you guys move to the beat of your own drum but I would have thought the M.E. would have been out here by now."

"He tends to run behind. Is this your first body, Miles?"

He swallowed. "First suicide." He thumbed over his shoulder. "Riley over there has dealt with a few deaths, senior citizens and whatnot, and that guy that shot his landlord last year but that's about it. Unless he's not telling me something."

"Miles here has been with the department, what is it? One year now?" Baker said glancing at Skylar.

"That's right."

"This is Reid's first day."

"Oh hey, pleased to meet you," Miles said, stepping forward looking to shake hands with her. He was still wearing dirty latex gloves. She declined. He looked down then realized. "Okay, well, should I leave you to it?"

"If you want, Miles. I'm sure your buddy over there needs someone to hold his hand."

He fumbled with his duty belt and turned and headed back over to the kid and his mother.

"Amateurs," Baker said.

While he was saying that and continuing to observe the body, Skylar snapped on gloves and went over to the truck. She roamed around it looking at the tracks and peered in through the window. There was an open pack of cigarettes on the seat, an empty bottle of Jack Daniel's, and a partially open letter where the first line stated — "If you have found my body, please know that I couldn't live anymore." The rest was hidden by a fold.

On the floor of the truck was a gun. She turned back to Baker.

"Any wounds on him beyond his head being missing?"

"Leeches, but that's it."

She walked back over to the body and crouched down beside Baker. He cast her a sideways glance, then took out his notepad. "Well, from what it looks like, it's a pretty straightforward case. Once we find out who it is, we'll notify the family and let them know that it was a suicide."

Baker stretched out his back.

"Where are his shoes? And why are his socks as clean as a whistle?"

Baker turned. "I wouldn't exactly call them clean."

"White socks, a muddy swamp. Sure they get soaked when you're in the water but if you take off your shoes before you walk over, this ground is going to darken up the bottoms real bad, same goes if he took them off once in the water. And why even bother removing them if you're going to kill yourself? Second, seems a little odd that if you were going to off yourself, you would steal a truck, walk into the swamp and leave a gun on the floor of the truck."

"Perhaps he planned on shooting himself."

"Possible. Then why not? Seems it would be a hell of a lot easier than to drown yourself."

Harvey studied her intently. "And you would know?" he paused. "Look, maybe he got here and realized he forgot the bullets. Or he drank so much he forgot and wandered down to the water and accidentally fell in."

"And what about the head? I'm no gator expert but I'm pretty damn sure they aren't picky or that clean." She lifted the tarp and pointed to the area around what would have been his neck. It wasn't exactly clean, but she had a point. "Then again, maybe it didn't like the taste."

"Miles, a quick word," Skylar bellowed. Baker looked at her and frowned.

The officer jogged over and adjusted his duty belt which appeared to be slipping.

"Did you take off his shoes?"

He glanced down at the body. "No, that's how they were when we dragged him out."

"Face up or face down?" Skylar said not even looking at him but focusing on the body.

"What? He didn't have a head."

"I know that, I'm referring to the body. Was the DOA facing up or down when you found him?"

"Um. Face up."

Skylar made a clucking sound with her tongue and brought a hand up to her chin. "Interesting."

"You care to elaborate?" Baker asked.

"I've dealt with floaters before. Once the body is exposed to water it changes, and then when rigor mortis sets in, it causes most bodies to float face down, not face up."

"What are you suggesting?"

"I'm not suggesting anything. I'm just saying that it's rare in accidental drowning cases to have a victim floating face up, especially if he'd been drinking."

"Maybe he wasn't drunk. We won't know much until the M.E. can take a look at the body, check for water in the lungs, see how long he's been in the swamp and do a toxicology report."

Skylar stood up and backed up a little, she turned and headed over to the truck while Miles and Baker looked on, then she peered into the back of the truck and took a hold of a tire iron. Without saying a word, she strolled around to the passenger side and cracked the side of the window, shattering the glass all over the seat.

"Reid, what the hell do you think you're doing? I was going to have a locksmith come out."

"And waste all that time and money?"

"Money? You know how much that is going to cost the department? Never mind the fact there could have been prints all over that damn window."

"Highly unlikely."

She wasn't listening to him, she reached inside. Still wearing gloves, she took a photo of the scene with her phone before picking up the letter. The suicide letter wasn't long, a few paragraphs at most. Nothing unusual about it.

"Well I think we have a name for our John Doe."

Harvey shook his head. "I can't believe you busted inside."

"Ted Sampson."

Baker coughed. "What did you say?"

She turned and handed him the letter. "It's signed, Ted Sampson. You know him?"

"Yeah. That's our M.E."

Chapter 4

Initially Baker thought they were going to have to get a medical examiner down from Gadsden County but after calling the Franklin County Medical Examiner and Coroner's Office he learned that Sampson had taken on an assistant. Baker hit the end call button on his cell phone and ran a hand through his hair.

"Well, looks like we are in luck. I thought we were going to have to wait an hour and a half to get someone down from Gadsden but seems ol' Sampson here had an ace in his pocket. Some young kid will be handling it. I do hope she's as good as Sampson was and not some college intern."

Baker turned back to the body.

"I just don't get it. I knew Sampson real well. We were golf buddies. Every two weeks we'd hit the green. Hell, you couldn't get the guy to shut up. He told me about the time he wasted twenty grand at a casino in Miami behind his wife's back and even shared a story about his recent colonoscopy. I mean the guy was an open book. I would have heard about issues he was having."

"You're not still buying into the suicide theory, are you?"

"Well, we can't rule it out yet. But no, I don't want to believe it was a suicide, simply because I knew him too well. He had everything going for him. A good-paying job. A good-looking wife, and one kid. On the surface things looked fine. But who knows?"

"Was he a drinker?"

"Ted? No. I mean he had a couple with me but he knew his limit. See, here's what you need to know about this guy. He knew the ins and outs of a body. If anyone was going to give you heck over eating a burger, it would have been him. The guy was as clean as a whistle."

Skylar breathed in deep. "Well obviously not, or he wouldn't have ended up here."

Right then, they heard the sound of a vehicle approaching.

"Great, must be the M.E."

"I doubt it," Skylar said as they turned and saw a cruiser coming into view.

"Oh right, that's all we need, the odd couple."

Sure enough it was Deputies Hanson and Reznik.

"Listen, when they show up don't admit to breaking the window, okay?"

"But…"

Baker turned. "They will ride me over it from now until I retire."

She shrugged. "Fine." The doors opened, and they smirked as they got out. "What's the deal with them, anyway?"

Baker leaned in and whispered, "They were transfers in from Miami. They were there for ten years working on the vice squad and now they think they know it all. They're like Crockett and Tubbs, you know, from *Miami Vice*. Except they lack the finesse and brains that those two actors had. Now they offer their criminal investigative skills as and when needed." He stifled a laugh as they made their way over ducking under the yellow tape and moving around to not leave more footprints.

"Oliver Hanson, the tall, overly butch-looking guy, mid-thirties with a shaven face, used to be a hairdresser before he became a cop. Which explains why he looks like he's just stepped out of a fashion magazine. Guy doesn't leave the station without a comb. Now he thinks he's some kind of world-class photographer. Then you have Jevaun Reznik who is the complete opposite. He could use some manners. Guy drops F-bombs like they are going out of business. He's part Jamaican descent, says he was part of Delta Force but that's just crap. He was in the army for four years until he got a medical release for an injury he got running. Though he won't say that. He'll tell you it's shrapnel from having done two tours and coming under attack by the Afghans. The only war he's seen is in front of the TV watching *Game of Thrones*."

Baker chuckled to himself.

"How do you know all this?"

"The captain showed me their files over coffee one morning. Anyway, just watch and see how he changes his walk when I mention it."

"Hello boys! So Reznik, how's that leg treating you?"

Baker nudged Skylar, and she watched as Reznik went from walking normally to limping ever so slightly. "Ah you know, the darn thing has been acting up lately."

Skylar smiled.

"Well, well, Baker. I see you have this under control," Hanson said glancing around and sniffing like he was about to wrap up the case in a matter of hours. "What a circus. Now please tell me you have not messed up our crime scene."

"Your crime scene?"

"The department's crime scene," he said correcting himself and pulling up from around his neck a large camera. "I'm gonna need DNA, prints and…" he trailed off beginning to look a little shocked. He backed up as if expecting the ground to cave in. "Please tell me you have not been crisscrossing this scene and you've been sticking close to the tape."

"Yes, yes, Hanson. Don't worry, no one has messed up your crime scene."

"Good, as with all these vehicles on the scene, I was beginning to think that you had crushed some of the tire tracks. I'm guessing you've checked, right?"

"Actually we were just about to do that, we're taken over from Miles."

"I will want a word with them before they leave. You know, routine."

"What, you want to take a photo of them for your wall?"

"Bite me," Hanson said brushing past him.

"What do you mean for your wall?" Skylar asked as they ducked under the police tape and made their way over to a section of the muddy clearing where Miles and the Jennings family were.

"He has a wall at work where he keeps photos from cases that he's been involved in and cracked."

"So how many has he got?"

"About seventeen. Mostly from his time in Miami. It's the weirdest thing you will ever see. Like a shrine."

"Where's he keep it?"

"In his locker."

"And the captain knows about this?"

"Not exactly. I kind of think he's not harming anyone."

"But you have to admit it's a little odd."

He cast her a smile. "Get used to it, Reid, there are a lot of things that are odd about this county, and I'm not talking about the good folks but the underbelly of society that most don't even know exists."

Skylar got a sense that her time there was going to be stranger than she imagined.

"Miles, you want to introduce us?"

Miles turned to the boy and mother. "Laura, this is Detectives Baker and…"

"Reid," Skylar added.

The lady was in her early forties, her son couldn't have been more than fifteen years of age. She looked worn down by life. Her eyes had huge bags underneath and she could have used a few more pounds on her.

"Detectives," she said extending a hand.

"And you are?"

"Ricky Jennings," Miles said when the question hadn't been posed to him.

Baker turned and pursed his lips. "Okay, boys, I think you've done a great job. I'm sure Carrabelle needs you back there, fighting crime. If I have any questions, I'll be in touch, okay?"

Miles gave a nod and he and the other officer trudged back to their cruiser.

"Do you know how much longer we need to be here?" Laura asked. "We've answered all the officers' questions. I have a shift at the diner that I need to get back to."

"We won't keep you long, I just had a few questions."

Before he could ask them, Skylar jumped in with a few questions of her own.

"So just out of curiosity, Ricky. Why were you all the way out here?"

He was a ginger-haired kid with a lot of freckles all over his face. His cheeks went a deep red. He was wearing fishing gear and there was a skiff pulled up on the shore. "I always come out here."

"His father used to bring him out here."

"Oh yeah? And where is he now?"

"Dead."

"I'm sorry to hear that."

"I'm not," Laura said. She spat on the floor. "The man didn't know how to treat a woman. Fortunately the good lord saw to it to stop his heart before he could hurt any more people."

Skylar cut Baker a glance before studying Ricky's face. He looked nervous, agitated and was rubbing his hands together. She glanced at them and saw that his knuckles were all red.

"You get into a fight, Ricky?"

His eyes flicked to her and guilt spread across his face as plain as day.

Laura slapped him around the back of the head.

"Well answer her, boy."

"Hey, no need to hit the kid," Skylar said. Nothing riled her up more than seeing parents go heavy-handed on kids. She'd grown up in an environment like that. Although her father had been a New York police officer, it didn't mean he was against knocking back a few too many and then taking out his anger on Skylar.

"I got into a bit of a scuffle at school. Nothing serious."

"The kids bully him. Tell them what they say." She paused waiting but he seemed reluctant. "Well go on."

"They call me a faggot. And tell me to go kill myself."

Skylar breathed out hard. "Well, kids can be real mean. Sorry to hear that. Have you spoken with the school, Ms. Jennings?"

"Oh like that would do anything. The school is as much to blame. You know what they told me on the phone?" Before Skylar could reply, she continued, "Boys will be boys. That's it. Ain't that just a beauty? Boys will be boys." She shook her head and crossed her arms over in front of her busty chest. Laura was about five foot four, all chest and she was still sporting a hairstyle from the '80s. Though she looked like she wasn't taking care of her own body, Ricky had fared well. That was something Skylar had always been mindful of when she worked in the big city. Child neglect. It was more common than abuse. Parents would send their kids off to school without breakfast, without a coat and not pay out for dental treatment but they sure as heck could find money for alcohol every night.

"Well, if you need us to put you in contact with some resources in the town that assist with bullying, we can do that. There is help."

Laura screwed up her face as if Skylar was patronizing her. Skylar noticed how hard she was gripping Ricky's hand, to the point that it was almost changing color. She might have said something, except it could have just been stress.

Baker immediately used the dead space to jump in. "So Ricky... you want take us back to what happened this morning?"

"I came out here around six."

"How did you get your boat out here?" Skylar interjected.

"A buddy of mine stores it at his place not far from here."

"And who would that be?"

He hesitated to reply, his eyes flicked over to his mother and she gave a nod leading him through what he was meant to do. "Lars Jackson."

Baker scowled. "That name is familiar."

"He's from Eastpoint."

"I know. How do you know him?"

"Just a friend."

"How long have you known him?"

Again he turned to his mother.

"He's a friend of the family. A guy I've dated over the years. Okay? Him and Ricky bonded after the death of my husband. They meet up occasionally to go fishing in the swamp. Satisfied?"

"And do you mind me asking how your husband died?" Skylar asked.

"A gator got him while he was out fishing."

"I thought you said his heart stopped?"

"It did, after the gator got him."

"And he was out here by himself?"

"That's right," she replied.

"And his name was?"

"Tucker Jennings."

Skylar took down notes on her pad.

"What does it matter? My husband has nothing to do with this investigation. This is about someone we don't even know. My kid just happened to be out here. Heck, he could have said nothing and just come home but… well…"

"So you never remarried?" Skylar asked.

"No. I might at some point but it was only eight months ago."

"That's unfortunate. You look real torn up," Skylar said noting how unfeeling she sounded towards her late husband. It had been six months since losing Alex and there wasn't a day that went by she didn't think of him. Then again, he'd never laid a finger on her. Was this woman just showing the signs of having been in an abusive relationship?

"You have a number for Lars and an address?"

Laura sighed and reeled it off as Baker took it down.

"Okay, so continue, Ricky. You came out here at six. Did Lars stay here with you?"

"No, he had to work, but he said he was going to drop by in the evening to get me."

"So at what time did you find the body?"

"It must have been a little after eight. I was out here catching largemouth bass."

"You catch anything?" Skylar asked walking over to where he'd dragged the boat in. She looked inside and saw his fishing rod and a box where he kept his tackle and bait.

"Nothing," he replied walking over as if nervous about what she might find.

"I can't imagine fish out of a swamp would taste good?"

"Ah it's not bad. Tastes pretty good."

Baker stepped forward staring at his notepad. "Did you hear anyone else nearby? See any other vehicles?"

"Nah, nothing. All I saw was his body. I brought the boat in and walked out of the swamp until I got a signal on my cell and phoned home."

"That's when I called the department," Laura added. Skylar tossed a glance over her shoulder at her and nodded. Skylar looked over to the truck. The odd couple were going through the process of dusting for prints, well, Reznik was, Hanson was in the middle of doing what looked like the splits in an attempt to get some weird-angled shot of the truck. Skylar's eyebrow shot up. Baker was right, those two were weird.

"Is there anything you might have forgotten?" Baker asked

Ricky shook his head. Skylar couldn't help notice how he would look to his mother as if seeking direction.

"Two last questions," Skylar asked. "Was the body facing up or down when you came across him?"

"Up."

"And do you mind if we keep a hold of your boat and tackle for a while?"

"Why?" His nose scrunched up.

"Just procedure. Our team is going to want to run some checks on it."

Laura stepped forward. "I hope you aren't suggesting my kid had anything to do with this?"

Baker flung up his hands. "Oh, no, Laura, it's just procedure. He should have it back by the time the day is out." He reached into his pocket and pulled out a card. "Here's my card, if you can think of anything, no matter how small it might be, just give me a call. Okay?"

She nodded, slipped the card between her breasts and yanked on Ricky's arm, taking him back to their banged-up Ford truck. Skylar continued to eye her as she walked away. There was something about her she didn't like, but she couldn't put her finger on it.

"So what do you think?" Baker asked.

"Well… something definitely smells fishy," Skylar remarked.

Chapter 5

Notifying next of kin was a real bummer. It didn't matter how many times she'd done it, Skylar wasn't comfortable with it. It wasn't the act of telling them their loved one was dead that bothered her as much as it was wondering if they thought she was sincere.

"Have you ever laughed when notifying a family member?" Skylar asked popping a stick of gum into her mouth. It had become her replacement habit for nicotine since giving up smoking four years ago. Sometimes she'd plow her way through a pack a day.

"No." He screwed up his face in disbelief. "Why would I laugh?"

Harvey guided his SUV around the bumpy road and back out onto the main stretch of road that fed back into Carrabelle.

"Whoa, steady, I'm not saying I would. I'm just asking."

"Yeah, well, it seems like an odd question."

"I don't mean because you find it funny but it's like one of those moments, you know, where you shouldn't be laughing but you want to laugh because it just feels so damn uncomfortable."

He raised an eyebrow. "I don't have a clue what you mean."

"For instance. Five years ago, I was invited to this funeral for a woman that had been a friend of the family. Now I knew her since I was a kid, great lady, nothing bad to say about her. Anyway, her husband is a complete wreck. Sobbing his heart out and the family are all gathered around him. I go along to the funeral with a couple of friends and opt to select a seat in an area that I think will keep me out of the line of sight. Anyway, everyone's sitting there waiting for the service to begin and they have this soft music playing over the speakers to create some atmosphere. Well, for some reason, it suddenly switches to the Peanuts Theme Song; you know, from Charlie Brown, the one with real heavy piano, and whatnot. Well, as hard as I tried to keep it together it was just too much. You have to picture it. A real somber atmosphere with people weeping and then some upbeat, whimsical tune comes on, and all I can think about is that damn dog. Throw in the funky dance and the wide grin he makes, and I was having a hard job keeping it together. Eventually I excused myself."

"Well whatever you're thinking, don't. Please, do not laugh."

"Calm down. I'm not saying I will, it's just I find myself steering towards humor when things are too serious."

"Well, steer in another direction. For God's sake, Reid, this is a man's life. I knew him."

She shrugged. "Okay, okay. I get it."

There was silence for a second or two.

"But what if…"

"NO!" he told her. "No what-ifs. If you don't think you can handle this, you stay outside while I go speak with her. I know his wife well and the last thing she needs is a cop acting like a laughing hyena."

Silence stretched between them for the rest of the journey. As the road wound its way down into Carrabelle, she knew it was going to take a while to adjust to the different pace, and kind of people that inhabited the area. Working on the task force, they shared a similar sense of humor. Cops called it dark humor. It was a coping mechanism that many cops ended up getting. She recalled the first time she heard about it from one of her academy instructors. At first she was mortified that anyone could find humor after being called out to a homicide or a freak accident but the longer she did the job, she started to see how it developed.

The town itself was a stark contrast to the big city living she was used to. Scot referred to Carrabelle as Old Florida when he was trying to sell her on it. It was the reason he'd bought a boat and had it moored there. It was a slower pace of life — a haven for anyone looking to escape, and a gateway to the Gulf of Mexico for offshore fishing and boating. In fact he said it would be perfect for her as the folks were the kind of people that loved coastal living but shied away from large crowds. There were no high-rise hotels, condominiums blocking the ocean view or roads clogged with four-lane traffic, it was just endless white-sand beaches, rich river marshes, diverse wildlife and small-town dwellings nestled within 750,000 acres of state and national forest.

The charming town that was considered Florida's best-kept secret, boasted a population of 2,700. Most were homegrown residents. In the short time Skylar had been there she'd found it easy to integrate with the locals that she came across in the coffee shop, neighborhood bars and restaurants. They struck her as unpretentious, warm and friendly. Harvey spoke of a darker underbelly, one that even most locals weren't aware of, and now she was beginning to get a sense that there was more to the town than what met the eye. Different homes shot by in her peripheral vision, blurring into the landscape. Like any small coastal town, it was filled with a balance of working class residents and those on the poverty line.

Neighborhoods varied from clapboard abodes, townhomes with wraparound porches to seedy trailers.

There were really only a few ways to access the hidden town, and that was by boat, US-98 along the coast, or south on State Highway 67 through the forest. The town had a grocery store, a pharmacy and couple of convenience stores, a hardware store, a gift shop and an old post office. Carrabelle offered little in the way of glitz and glamor — the kind of nightlife that might be found in the heavily populated regions of Florida.

Skylar brought a window down and inhaled the salty air, wondering how long it would take to get used to it. Although she enjoyed being away from the hustle and bustle, the neon lights and twenty-four-hour service that New York dripped, she wasn't sure if the job would offer her the kind of pace she thrived on.

She shot Harvey a glance out the corner of her eye, he was humming away to some classical tune, his fingers moving like a conductor's fingers.

Her mind drifted.

After leaving the U.S. Marshals, she'd spent the first few months locked away in her apartment until one day Scot showed up and tore the curtains open, flooding her dingy abode with natural light before telling her that enough was enough.

"Jesus, Skylar," he said taking in the sight of her messy apartment. Garbage was overflowing from the bins, the sink was full, the cupboards and fridge bare and there were several empty takeout boxes dotted around the room. "Time to get up. This isn't doing you any good. I miss Alex as much as you do but he wouldn't want this for you. I sure as hell don't. C'mon, up you get," he said tugging at the quilt she had buried herself in. "When was the last time you left this apartment?" He tore off the blanket, and she huddled up into a ball and pulled a pillow over her head. She didn't reply, except to wave him away like an annoying fly. She could hear him clearing up boxes and tossing several empty bottles of Jack Daniel's into black trash bags.

"Scot, just leave it."

"Nope. You are going to get up, take a shower if I have to

drag you in there with your clothes on."

"What does it matter to you?"

"Why does it matter?" He scoffed. "I swear, Skylar, I thought you were stronger than this. I get it. Alex's gone. I lost a lot of good friends in that explosion too but that's the risk we take with this job. Alex knew that, so do you. But hiding away isn't going to help. Now get up."

Scot and Alex had been best of friends. They'd gone through the academy together and though Alex wasn't on the same task force as Skylar, he'd always made a point to have Scot keep an eye out for her. Not that she needed help. In fact she'd saved his ass more times than he'd saved hers. She felt him clasp her hand and tug her up. She acted like a dead weight hoping he would get frustrated, curse and leave. But that wasn't him. He pulled her up and over his shoulder and carried her into the bathroom where he plunked her down in the bath. All she was wearing was panties and a white stained T-shirt. She heard the faucet turn and the next second, freezing cold water covered her. She gasped, and he burst out laughing. "That's it. Wake up. Life is shocking. Get *used to it."*

"Just go away, Scot."

He sat on the toilet seat and crossed his legs. "Nope. Shower up, get dressed, I'm taking you out for breakfast. I have a proposition for you. I think you'll like it."

"I don't want to deal with this."

"Well you are going to have to as I'm not going anywhere."

She turned off the faucet and stood there dripping wet, her tears mixing with the water until even he could tell that whatever fight she had left was gone. Scot got up and took a hold of her by the arms.

"Skylar. I miss him too. I would do anything to have him back here but he's gone."

"I lost the baby," She blurted it out. Her words cut through the air.

"What?"

"I had a miscarriage. I didn't even get the chance to tell him I was pregnant."

The doctor believed the stress of losing Alex played a role.

She had been eight weeks into the pregnancy before she realized. The doctor said it wasn't uncommon for women to not realize they were pregnant.

Harvey slammed on the brakes shaking Skylar out of the past. He brought his window down and shouted at some kid that had cycled out in front of them nearly causing an accident.

"Billy Taylor, I know where you live!"

Skylar laughed. "Steady, Harvey, you might burst a blood vessel."

"Damn kids."

"You were one once."

"Yeah but I had the common sense not to cross the street without looking."

Ted Sampson's residence was just off Gulf Avenue. It looped around the south section of Carrabelle and connected with US-98. It was a modest one-story home with palm trees in the front yard and a white picket fence. It was a stone's throw away from one of the three rivers that converged at Carrabelle and connected with the Gulf of Mexico. They veered into the tranquil beachfront setting, their tires crunching over sand and gravel as they made their way up to the pale gray clapboard home. A dark SUV was parked outside, near a separate garage. Beyond the home was a dock that extended out forty feet into the pristine waters of the Gulf, which glistened under a cloudless sky.

"You said he had kids?"

"One, a boy. Good kid too."

"How old?"

"Nine."

Skylar shook her head despondently. It was one thing to lose a husband but for a kid to have his father torn out of his world at such a young age was unforgiveable.

"Now listen up, Skylar, if you're not up to this I would understand."

He was trying to talk her out of going in with him. The guy was used to working alone, and she'd already sensed his reluctance to have her as a partner. She wasn't particularly keen on it either but they both had to deal with it. "I'll follow your lead, how's that sound?" She mimicked zipping her lips if only to put his mind at rest.

He narrowed his eyes and pushed out of the vehicle. The screen door to the home opened long before they reached it. The woman that stood in the doorway was about five ten, with fiery red hair and green eyes. She was wearing a thin blouse, a pair of white shorts and sandals.

"Harvey? What are you doing here?"

She looked confused and cast her gaze beyond his SUV.

"Rachel. You think we can go inside?" he suggested. Her demeanor changed like the sun being swallowed by dark clouds. An expression of concern flickered on her face as she nodded and led them into the hardwood floor hallway. Nothing inside looked worn, or weathered. No paint chipped, or disorder to the home. Skylar wiped her feet on a welcome mat. The fresh smell of bacon permeated the air. Farther down the corridor Skylar spotted a young boy sitting at a breakfast counter. Harvey suggested they step into the living room.

"What is it, Harvey?"

Over the course of the next five minutes he brought her up to speed on what they'd discovered. Tears streaked her cheeks while her son Jaden stood by the door fumbling with a Frisbee. Their golden retriever sat by his feet looking as curious as he was.

The first thing that struck her was the abundant display of photos gracing the walls. Most were from family vacations. Happier days, free from the horror that had befallen them. She noticed one with Jaden and Ted fishing. Both were wearing shorts and a T-shirt, holding up large bass and grinning — a triumphant moment that indicated a close relationship and a mutual love of the outdoors. It was only now that she could put a face to the body she'd seen earlier. He was partially balding, and most of the hair he had was full of silver flecks.

Skylar noticed an office adjacent to the living room. The sliding glass doors were closed but she could make out a large mahogany desk and a library of books on shelves behind it. It had always interested her how other people lived. What they did with their time when their careers weren't eating into their existence.

All the furniture in the room had that crisp new look to it as though she'd just stepped into a home store that had décor on display. Nothing seemed out of place. On a table were four home and garden magazines fanned out as if presented that way on purpose. She had to wonder if anyone even used the room. The TV didn't have a spot of dust on it. It seemed almost unnatural, then again it was common for folks to have one living area for guests and another for family — a way to keep order and disorder apart.

Rachel sat with her knees together, picking at her finger nervously. She couldn't have been a day over forty-four. Certainly younger than Ted. She sneezed into a tissue and wiped away mascara from her cheeks.

"It doesn't make any sense. He wouldn't have done this. You know that, Harvey."

Harvey nodded, a look of sympathy on his face. Skylar leaned against a wall and observed. She was keen to see how Harvey handled himself as an officer. From the small amount of time they'd been together, she got a sense that he was cautious and caring. Though perceptions could be deceiving.

"Rachel, I understand but we have to consider it as a possibility. I knew him well, and I didn't see this coming but there are many who have lost loved ones to suicide that didn't see it coming. Now I know you might not want to discuss this but I have to bring it up. Was he taking any medication? Anything that might have caused him to think differently?"

"He'd been to see his doctor mainly over stress but he wasn't suffering from depression if that's what you're asking." She rose to her feet and shook her head. "Look, can I get you some coffee? I really need some coffee."

Harvey glanced at Skylar and she shrugged. It was kind of an odd question to ask in the middle of questioning but she gave a nod. Rachel hurried away into the kitchen and she continued to talk while she made coffee. Jaden stared at both of them without saying a word. Skylar walked over to him. He had this shocked look on his face as though he couldn't comprehend what he was hearing as though it was all a dream.

"What's your dog's name?"

"Bella."

Skylar crouched down and ran a hand over the dog's head and scratched under her chin. "Cute name. You play Frisbee much?"

"Yeah, usually with my dad." Skylar's heart sank. She wasn't sure how to reply to that. Fortunately Rachel returned with a tray and set it down. She returned to her seat.

"Look, is there anyone we can call to come and be with you?" Harvey asked.

She shrugged. "My sister."

Harvey reached for a cup of coffee and passed it to Skylar. For a minute or two they filled their cups with milk and sugar and tried to act as if they weren't there on a death notification. After a few awkward moments of silence Harvey continued, "Does he keep his medication here?"

"Yeah, I can get it for you."

She got up and headed off down the hallway and returned a moment later with two brown plastic bottles with white labeling. Harvey glanced at them before stuffing them in his pocket.

"You mind me asking if he spoke about what stress he was under? Was it work related?"

"He said it was a number of things that had been piling up and he wasn't able to sleep at night. I'd wake up in the middle of the night and find him working away on his computer."

"When did that start?"

"Working away or not sleeping?"

"Both," Harvey said.

"Maybe six months."

"Any pressure with finances?"

She squeezed her eyelids and wiped at the corner of her face as a tear trickled down. "Nothing out of the ordinary. I mean, he always felt like we weren't earning enough but everyone thinks that way, right?"

That struck Skylar as odd being as the average chief medical examiner earned approximately $208,000 a year in Florida. That wasn't anything to sneeze at and it certainly explained why the contents of their home looked new. Then again, some people lived beyond their means and the fact that Harvey had mentioned him blowing twenty grand behind his wife's back in Las Vegas, made her wonder if he had a gambling habit.

Skylar had to ask. "Rachel, did Ted travel to Miami often?"

She glanced up at her. "No, I mean, he went there a few times. Said it was related to business. Um, training, you know. Updating his skills and whatnot but that was only a couple of times a year."

Harvey circled back to the stress. "Other than the times I went out with him, was there anything about his regular day-to-day activities that stands out to you? A change in routine? New friends?"

"I didn't keep track of his every move, Harvey. Most

days when he came home, he sat in front of the TV, drank a couple of beers and passed out. Other nights, he would retreat to his study. Sometimes he headed out to the store, or went out for drinks with friends."

"Friends?"

She shrugged. "Work friends."

"He ever have them over for dinner?"

"Nope. But I did ask. But he would just say that the conversation would bore me because it was work related."

Harvey nodded. "I have to ask, Rachel. Did Ted ever attempt to take his own life?"

Her eyes widened as if she couldn't believe he was asking.

"It's because of the note."

Her eyes darted down. "He spoke about it. He'd talk about how he didn't know what he was going to do when he retired, and whether or not we would have enough money to survive."

"Was money tight?"

"I don't think it was, but he was always concerned that

there was not enough or that something was going to happen and we would be scraping the bottom of the barrel. Anyway, he mentioned a few times that he was in a very dark place in his head and wanting to be done with everything but that's when I told him to go and see a doctor. I said they could help with the stress and give him something for it. He did." She paused. "Actually it wasn't long after that. Maybe two weeks later he started to seem optimistic. You know, like a shift had occurred. I just assumed it was the medication he was taking, but he said that he was investing in a new venture — an online gambling website. A local company called Royal City."

Skylar looked at Harvey and she had a sense that they were thinking the same thing.

"Anyway, he seemed like a different guy. He was full of energy when he got home from work, he even said he wasn't taking his medication anymore." She gave a strained smile.

"And when did you last see or speak to Ted?" Harvey asked.

"Last night. He phoned to say he was going to be running a little late and that he wouldn't be able to make dinner. It was my mother's eightieth birthday. We were going to celebrate with family."

"At home?"

"No, at my mother's house."

"So that's where you were last night?"

"Yeah, Jaden and I stayed there for the evening to keep her company. I lost my father a few years back and so my mother has been a bag of nerves since."

Silence stretched between them for a few minutes as they sat and drank their coffee.

"Rachel, was it common for Ted to run late?"

"I wouldn't say it was common, but it occurred. Yeah."

"And he didn't elaborate beyond that?"

"No."

Skylar continued to take down notes. "And so he wasn't seeing anyone on the side?"

Harvey shot her a look, and she rephrased it.

"I mean, you wouldn't think Ted was the type of man that he would have played around on you?"

Rachel's features hardened. "No. If you knew him, you would know he wouldn't do that."

"Sorry, I had to ask," Skylar said before glancing at Harvey who rolled his eyes. "So beyond that conversation there was nothing else out of the ordinary?"

"Well, he had recently mentioned moving to Colorado but you know it was one of those things he said as a passing comment over dinner. He thought it would be nice to be closer to his family."

"When did he ask that?" Harvey asked.

"Last week, why?"

Harvey frowned and Skylar could see he was puzzled by it. She was keen to find out what he knew. Had Ted told him something that contradicted him wanting to move? Harvey leaned forward and set his coffee cup down.

"Before we leave, if you could give us the names and numbers of those that were at the dinner last night. It's just routine. I'll need to follow up with them."

Rachel nodded and went off to get her phone.

***

It didn't take long to verify her alibi. While Harvey made the calls, Skylar followed up with the coroner's office to establish a timeline of when Ted finished his shift, she then cross-checked that with when Rachel had been expecting him and something didn't add up. According to his assistant he left work at his normal time which meant he went somewhere else, the question was where?

After arranging to have her sister come and stay with her, Rachel led them into his study so they could browse his computer. The only problem was, he'd set up a password on both his desktop and laptop, which meant they weren't going to be able to go through it, and Rachel had no idea what the password was.

"Sorry I can't be any further help. He tended to keep things to himself."

Skylar was looking at Rachel but could see Jaden out

the corner of her eye lingering nearby. When there was a knock at the door and she went off to answer it, Harvey phoned through to the department to find out if Axl was around.

"Who's Axl?"

Harvey put the phone in the crook of his neck to answer her while they had him on hold.

"The county's computer whiz kid. I swear he could tear a laptop apart and put it back together with his eyes closed. He doesn't work for the department per se, but he runs a computer support and services company in town so the department calls him from time to time to help out with the network and odd jobs."

"Why don't they just hire him?"

"Department doesn't have the budget or the demand. Though he spends more time hanging around down at the station than he does at his own store. Hires others to do the mundane work and he has managed to land himself contracts with different small police departments in the area. I guess you could say he's a traveling brain."

She nodded and looked over to Jaden who was tossing a ball around in his hand and glancing into the study. Even though he was aware that his father wasn't coming home, he seemed to be handling the news better than his mother.

"Dog Island," he muttered in almost a whisper.

"What?"

"Try Dog Island. It was his favorite place to fish."

Skylar squinted and was about to tap Harvey who was discussing the latest findings with another officer over the phone but instead she leaned in and tapped it in herself. As soon as she hit enter, lo-and-behold it logged in. "Well I never." She glanced up, and the kid was no longer there. She could hear Rachel calling to him to come and say hello to his auntie.

"Harvey."

He turned and frowned. "Davis, I'll call you back." He hung up and looked at her. "Okay, you want to tell me how you did that?"

"The kid."

Harvey looked out of the room and then leaned over her as she started with the most obvious — email. It would take a while as he hadn't cleared out his email and there were thousands of read emails.

"Check his Internet history."

"Hold on."

"And check…"

Skylar swiveled in her seat. "You want to do this?"

He tossed his hands. "I'm just saying."

She returned to scanning through messages he'd received in the last few days before he died. Skylar clicked on one that came from a realtor.

Hi, Mr. Sampson, it was good to speak on the phone regarding your search for a property. I have some good news. The owners of the three-bedroom home accepted your offer and the closing date would work with them. All I need you to do is sign off on a few more documents, which I have attached, and we can get the ball rolling. You could be in the house as early as next month. If you have any further questions, please feel free to phone me.

Terri Moulton

ReMax Realty

"Well how about that? Sounds like Ted wasn't just making a passing comment to his wife. Seems he was ready to up and move within the month? You want to check with her and find out if she knew about this?" Skylar asked.

Harvey nodded and went to find her. Meanwhile Skylar continued searching. There was a ton of spam from financial companies and realtors, along with personal emails from family and even one from Harvey. She did a search using the keyword phrase "Royal City." About a hundred and fifty emails came up. She began going through some of the earliest ones. They were mostly related to his online gambling and money that he'd won. Several were newsletters and one was seeking investors. She moved on to sent emails and discovered some communication showing a serious interest in the company and requesting to meet with the founder and CEO, William Akitt. Then she located a reply that gave a date and time. At the bottom was the address for Royal City. Skylar took a second to print it off before Harvey returned.

"Rachel said she didn't know about any purchase and that he made it sound as if he was just thinking about it."

Skylar leaned back in her seat. "Take a look at this," she tossed the printout across the table and Harvey scooped it up. "Seems a little odd, don't you think, that he would get involved with some company and then want to up and move within a matter of a month?"

Harvey shook his head. "He never told me anything about this."

"Did he mention Busty Asians too?"

She turned the monitor around and flashed some adult website. "I pulled up his Internet history. Seems the man had a taste for the Orient."

"Dear God, and I thought I knew him."

"Come on, Harvey, at a glance of his history, he visited

social media, sports, news, fishing and porn sites, which represents 99% of men around the world, and as for the other 1%, they're lying and deleting their history. As you know, people wear all kinds of masks, Harv," she said tapping the table with her fingers. "Which raises another point that we should consider. As much as you like to think you know Rachel, we should probably look into what kind of life insurance Ted had. She might have been at that birthday bash but that doesn't mean she didn't hire someone to rub him out."

"Are you always this brash?"

"Only when I haven't had my second cup of coffee." She sniffed. "Oh, and we should probably see if we can obtain some financial records as that might also give us a picture of what has been going on over the past year."

"Hold on, Skylar. Until we can prove otherwise, this is going to be considered a suicide, not murder."

"And?"

"Well, requesting financial records. I think we are going to have to cut our way through some serious red tape to get that."

"Just ask her, Harvey. You'll be surprised at what people will willingly hand over."

"I'm guessing you've had a lot of experience with this," he replied.

"By the way I looked into the timeline of when he left his work and he didn't stay late which means he must have had some meeting planned and my bet is on Royal City."

Harvey shifted his weight from one foot to the next. "Something smells fishy? A taste for the Orient, your bet is on Royal City? Am I going to endure your puns every day?"

She smirked, and she tapped him on the chest. "That depends on how long I can endure you."

"Endure me?"

He followed her out.

"Listen, we're going to need one of the officers to go through the rest of the computer, also check his laptop. This guy never deleted a damn thing. His computer history stems back two years. Either he was a techno neophyte or a digital hoarder, either way he's left some nice digital footprints that might provide some clues to what he was up to on that final day but it's going to take a while to go through it, and…"

"And why can't you do it?"

She cast a glance at her watch. "Me? I have an appointment."

"With who?"

"A therapist."

"I should have figured," he said. "But what about the investigation?"

"It's lunch time, Harv, go buy a sub, eat a donut, drink coffee, do whatever cops do."

He tossed a hand in the air. Skylar turned and regarded him with a serious look. She knew she had issues but wasn't aware they were so obvious. The first few months after getting out of the U.S. Marshals her therapy amounted to a bottle of Jack Daniel's and microwave dinners until Scot pulled her out of her slump and tried to get her back into the land of the living. So much about what had occurred had torn her up, it was hard to face one tragedy but two? It cut her to the core and for the longest time she didn't even want to face the world. But after arriving in Florida, she was beginning to think that Scot was right. Her entire career she'd had her foot on the accelerator, never slowing down to admire the world around her. Losing Alex and having a miscarriage had slammed on the brakes in a violent manner. She felt like she was dealing with some emotional whiplash and there were only a few ways through it. One was getting out there, working again and seeing that life still continued, and the other was talking about it — that was the part she wasn't too good at. It was easier to deflect, to make light of serious situations, than face what was going on inside of her. Scot had put her in touch with a therapist, and in many ways gone to bat for her with the department, calling in a favor. Had it not been for him, she'd still be curled up in a ball inside her New York apartment surrounded by months-old trash.

Chapter 6

It was to be her first therapy session. Scot had made arrangements for her to see Dr. Ben Walker several months ago but after arriving she just couldn't bring herself to open up to a complete stranger. It seemed too cold, besides, she couldn't help but wonder how it would be of any benefit, so she just kept canceling her appointments. Now she figured that any other therapist might have become annoyed and told her to forget booking another appointment. He didn't. Instead, he would leave the same message with her voicemail.

"Ms. Reid, this is Dr. Ben Walker. I hope you're well. It appears you didn't show for your appointment. I've booked you in for the same time, next week. I look forward to seeing you. Call my office if this date doesn't work for you and we can arrange a more convenient time."

She had to give it to him, he was persistent.

Skylar eased off the gas as she pulled into a space in front of his home, which he used for his therapist service. It was a beautiful place reminiscent of a Mediterranean house with a shallow, sloping tiled roof and verandas. The front was faced with white wood and it had lots of windows with turquoise shutters to allow a cool breeze to flow through the home. It had a two-car garage, and a perfectly landscaped yard with palm trees either side of the walkway.

She sat in his driveway for several minutes contemplating driving away. The truck idled, and she was certain she saw someone peek out from behind white drapes. *Great, he's probably seen me. Now I can't drive away.* She shut off the engine, then started it back up again. This occurred three times before she told herself to get a grip and go in. It was just a half-hour session. Nothing to get freaked out about. Worse-case scenario she would just sit there in silence or give him a bag of lies.

Skylar smoothed out her clothing and checked her hair in the side mirror before heading up to the door. The temperature outside had already climbed to an uncomfortable 85 degrees. The air was hot and humid. She didn't have to knock as there was a sign on the door that instructed her to let herself in and go into the study on the left. At the assigned time, the session would begin. Skylar entered and was immediately greeted by a Labrador retriever. The dog ambled over and she hunched over to scratch his chin. As she did, she took in the sight of the foyer. There was a gorgeous chandelier, hardwood floors and a staircase that disappeared up to a powder room. The two-car garage was to her right and peering farther into the house she could just make out a living room. She entered the study and noted how well designed the place was. It had a clean and fresh look to it with touches of beach décor. There was a white sofa on the left with a mirror above it, and a dark brown wicker basket acting as a table in the center of the room, below that was an area rug with a shell design on it. To the left of the sofa was a desk with a Mac laptop, a lamp and a bowl full of shells. There was a photo on the side table of a kid who looked to be around ten years of age. He was in baseball gear and behind him was a Little League team.

She immediately felt a sense of peace. Skylar took a seat and gazed around. A light breeze blew in through the window making the room feel airy and light. Whoever had designed the place definitely knew a thing or two about creating a relaxed atmosphere.

A clock ticked as she waited for her noon session to start. There was still about four minutes until it began. She assumed he would show up early to introduce himself and whatnot. She had in her mind some old guy with a paunch looking like Mister Rogers. A soothing voice that would repeat everything she said back to her. Oh, she was all too familiar with psychologists. The U.S. Marshals had them available for anyone who felt they needed to talk about what they were seeing on a day-to-day basis. Except, everyone viewed going to one as a sign of weakness, maybe that was because law enforcement still had an old boys' club mentality. Perhaps that's why she'd never taken advantage of the free resource. Skylar glanced at the clock — two minutes. Where was he? She leaned forward and peered around the door before looking at the magazines on the table in front of her which were to do with home décor. She readjusted herself feeling a little uncomfortable. Whatever peace she felt when she walked in had now been replaced by a sense of discomfort. She rolled her neck around feeling tension building up. One more minute passed, and she began questioning if she should have shown up. *Leave. Get up. Go now. He won't even know you arrived. You don't need this. You can handle this all by yourself. You don't have a problem. Honestly, Skylar, do you think this man has the answers?* Her mind wouldn't let up. Her eyes darted to the clock, now she was looking at the second hand ticking over. Thirty seconds left. She hopped up and had just made it to the door when she bumped into him coming in.

"Oh, sorry!"

She lifted her eyes, and he smiled.

"You must be Skylar Reid. Dr. Ben Walker." He put

out his hand at a downward angle because they were so close. Skylar backed up and cleared her throat before shaking it.

"I was just going to get a bottle of water from my truck."

"Sure you were," he made a motion to the sofa. "Take a seat. I'll get you a bottle."

He turned around and headed off, then within a matter of seconds was back. Had he run? He was obviously determined to make sure she didn't dash out. He closed the door behind him and her eyes roamed over him. He wasn't what she'd imagined. Far from it. In fact, he looked as if he'd just stepped out of a *GQ* magazine. He was just shy of six foot, average build, designer stubble and glasses, though they didn't make him look like a nerd, more like, intelligent? He had a full head of styled dark hair though there were a few silver flecks at the temples. He was wearing a dark denim shirt, gray casual pants and brown shoes. In his hand was an iPad.

He handed her the bottle of water covered in

condensation.

"Well, it's good to finally meet. I assumed you'd eventually show up when you were ready."

"Actually I was just…"

"… about to leave?" He gave a warm smile that immediately put her at ease.

She didn't respond but sank back into the sofa just wanting to get on with it. He tapped a timer on the side and leaned back in his chair. "So how are you settling into Carrabelle?"

"Oh, it's just peachy."

She looked around.

"You know if you want to leave the door is there. I'm just saying."

She picked at a loose thread on her jeans. "No, I'm fine."

He glanced down at his iPad. "Scot sent over your profile."

"He did?"

"He obviously cares for you."

She shifted in her seat and got a serious look on her face. "Just out of curiosity, how do you know Scot? Did he just randomly pick you out of the Yellow Pages?"

"No, we go way back. We volunteered for Victim Support, back when he was only eyeing the U.S. Marshals. He went his way, I went mine. But we're still good friends."

She nodded and leaned back crossing her legs and acting disinterested. She was listening, but she was hoping that eventually he would realize that he didn't have the answers and he'd direct her elsewhere. It wasn't that she was trying to be an ass, but talking with anyone who thought they could solve her problems seemed like madness.

He glanced down at the iPad and ran his finger over it.

"So you did nine years with the New York Police Department, and eight with the Marshals, I imagine you saw a lot of shocking things?"

She glanced at the photo of the kid, shifting the topic

away from her. "Is that your son?"

His lip curled up, and he reached across and turned it. When he did, she noticed there was no ring on his finger and no tan line that would indicate he'd removed it. "It is. His name's Sam. Did you always want a child?"

The second he said it, her eyes cast down, and she looked at her watch.

"You know, ignoring the pain is not going to make it go away. And eventually the department is going to ask how you are doing."

"Hold on a second. The department?"

"Yeah. I often work with officers from the Carrabelle police and the surrounding counties. That's why Scot thought I'd be a good fit for what you are going through."

"What I'm going through? What am I going through, Dr. Walker?"

"You can call me Ben."

"Yeah, I think we are done here," she said getting up.

"Skylar," Ben said rising to his feet. "I think you may have misunderstood. Everything that is shared within these four walls, is held in the strictest confidence. However, if you don't find some way of dealing with the pain, it's going to show up in your work and then... the department is going to be asking questions. That's what I meant."

She stared back at him with her hand on the door, ready to leave.

"Please. Let's at least finish the session."

She released the handle and returned to her seat.

"What do you want to know?"

"Tell me about Alex."

***

Later, Harvey was in the lunchroom listening to Diana Fletcher, a motivational speaker. Elizabeth had bought her entire collection. It was meant to help with the stress. His eyes were closed, and he was munching away on an egg sandwich when he felt one of the earbuds yanked from his ear. His eyes snapped open to find Skylar shoving one in her ear.

"Breathe in. Breathe out. Remember, you are in

control of your peace."

"Oh Harv, you don't actually buy into all that mumbo jumbo, do you?" She tossed back the earbud and went over to the coffee machine. She tossed in a few coins, and a cup dropped and it began churning away. "Let me guess, you also listen to Anthony Robbins, 'Unleash the Power Within.'"

"I would have you know Diana Fletcher is a world-renowned author and lecturer. My wife swears by it."

"Ah, so your wife bought it for you," she said taking out her coffee and sipping. "You do know they have drugs for stress?"

"You sound like you speak from experience," he said getting up and turning off the recording. "You know, I only get a short time to center myself in the afternoon and you just went and messed it up."

"No. C'mon." She glanced at her watch. "I've been gone nearly forty-five minutes. What have you been doing?"

He put away the Tupperware with the last few scraps

of his sandwich. "I've been trying to arrange an appointment to see the CEO of Royal City."

"An appointment? We're the cops, we don't need appointments."

"You do if you want to catch the guy when he's in. According to his secretary, he tends to be out on the road a lot. Something related to advertising and marketing and whatnot."

"By the way, any luck with the M.E. assistant?"

"She's looking over the body as we speak. It will probably take a couple of weeks to get back the toxicology report."

"Weeks? We don't have weeks. What's the gal's name?"

She headed towards the door hoping to speak with her.

"It's Jenna Madden but you aren't going to get anywhere. We'll have the autopsy report back but not the toxicology yet. In the meantime we need to find out the connection between Ted and this online gambling company. Something doesn't add up. You don't just go from depression to elation overnight unless you're bipolar. I got in contact with his doctor while you were at your session. Which reminds me. How did it go?"

"Peachy," she replied not wanting to get into it.

"Anyway, his doctor said he came in half a year ago complaining about stress and anxiety and not being able to sleep. The prescription he received has been renewed a few times and then he stopped getting it filled. So, it sounds like Rachel was telling the truth. As for a life insurance policy, everything checks out there. No changes made since it was taken out." He took a step back to give her some space. Skylar sipped on her coffee. "I also followed up with the realtor out in Colorado. Seems that Ted was in contact with them around a month after he got in contact with Royal City. He even made a trip out there to buy a house. Now either he was thinking of moving out there by himself or he was just withholding a lot from Rachel. So, that leads me back to Royal City. Was he trying to get away from something he got caught up in? We already know that he blew twenty grand behind her back. I'm having one of our guys go through his financial records to find out what kind of state they were in. I'm getting a sense that he hid a lot from Rachel."

"I wouldn't be surprised if he paid all the bills too. She might not even know how much is in the bank account. It happens in relationships."

"Not in mine it doesn't," Harvey said.

"You know, I've been thinking about that missing head. What if it didn't wind up inside one of those gators? What if he was bludgeoned to death somewhere else, and then they chopped his head off to make it look as if a gator had attacked him to hide the cause of death? Of course a gator may have taken it. The question is who did he see that night after work and where did he go?" Skylar tossed the rest of her coffee into the trash bin and grimaced. "Man, that stuff is nasty. I say we check camera footage from some of the stores nearby, maybe some of the bars and see if anyone caught him in town that night."

"We'll need a warrant."

"Damn, Harv, if you need that you're asking the wrong way."

"What? And how do you ask?"

"Come on, I'll show you."

Chapter 7

On the way over to check on CCTV footage from stores in the area, Harvey got a call from William Akitt's secretary to let him know that her boss was back. Harvey did a U-turn and headed towards the northeast of town. Royal City was located just a few blocks from the municipal complex on Grays Avenue. It was a stylish building made up of 80 percent glass and the rest was brick and steel. Outside was a courtyard with a fountain spouting water high into the air. Harvey pulled into the lot designated for customers and Royal City workers.

"They fought to keep this out of the town but obviously someone in high places managed to put it through. While it's not a casino, people don't like having this kind of thing in the town."

"Seems like an odd place to have a head office. I would have imagined Miami and gambling went together," Skylar said.

"Yeah but they're a low-key organization right now. A new upstart company probably wants to keep overhead low. Building something like this in Miami would cost a bundle. I'm sure once they turn over enough cash they will branch out, hopefully taking this eyesore out of the community."

Skylar got a sense the town resisted any form of change. Many small towns were like that. It wasn't a bad thing. Folks knew what they liked, and they wanted to keep it that way. She could respect that. As they hopped out, Skylar ran the back of her hand over her brow and gazed up at the burning sky. The heat was making beads of sweat trickle down her back. A single rogue cloud drifted until it disappeared. They crossed the lot and headed into the modern lobby that was synonymous with technology startups. It was like everyone was trying to model themselves after Google with the same selection of colors for décor. There were wooden benches and real trees inside. Cocoons off to the right had a cushioned booth inside along with a phone. It was like they were trying to appeal to five-year-olds and make work a fun place to be.

In front of them was a white front desk that was curved into an S shape and had colorful lava lamps in front of it. There was a glass of candy set on the top of the desk and a huge neon sign behind a lady sitting there that read: ROYAL CITY

On the walls were flat-screen TVs showing the latest online gambling games being played and money being lost and won in real time.

As they approached the front desk, a broad-shouldered man wearing a pinstripe suit came out of an office to the right. He quietly said something to the lady at the desk but was glancing at them as they got closer.

"Can I help you?" he asked.

"Detective Baker, and you would be?"

"Manning. Giles Manning."

Skylar stifled a laugh; she couldn't help find his introduction amusing. She muttered under her breath, "Bond. James Bond."

The man must have heard her as he shot her a dirty look.

"And you are?"

"Royal City's team manager. I oversee and make sure everything is running lickety-split."

Several people passed by holding boxes. There was an unusual number of boxes going in and out.

"Busy day for deliveries?"

"Yeah, it's been a bit manic around here over the past few months. We're still in the process of establishing and setting up the main office. It takes time."

"And would Ted Sampson have been involved in establishing it?"

"Sampson?" He frowned for a second. "Oh, you're referring to one of our investors. Sorry, we've had a lot of investors interested in helping us. Some are quiet and prefer to operate in the background but Ted, he was a real hands-on man."

"That he was. Care to elaborate?"

"He met with our CEO on a frequent basis, he liked to

have a say in how we were conducting business, upgrades to the website, etcetera. Sometimes he even helped in the warehouse out back."

"Warehouse? I wouldn't imagine you would have a need for one being as you're an online gambling service?" Skylar said.

"We have a store that offers products to our clients."

"Interesting, sell any heels? I've been thinking of buying a new pair," Skylar said walking towards the back room.

"Um, you're not allowed back there. It's only for staff."

"Oh come on now, you're not Google. What secrets would you be holding back?"

"I mean, you can't go back there without William's permission. Sorry, not my rules."

Both of them gazed around. "So you want to point us in the direction of William Akitt?"

"Um, I don't believe he is around right now."

Harvey chuckled and leaned over the desk. "Nancy, is

it?"

The female looked like a cardboard cutout. Her posture was near perfect. She had long dark flowing hair that looked like someone had flattened it with a road roller. Her specs were pointed, her teeth were overly bright, and she wore just the right amount of makeup.

"Yes, detective."

"It was you who phoned me, was it not?"

"Yes. He was here. Maybe he's stepped out."

"Or maybe he's out back, how about I just go back there and…"

Skylar slipped around Giles and headed down a long corridor that ended at a set of double doors. Giles took off after her protesting that he didn't want to lose his job.

She tapped him on the chest. "It's okay, Giles, I'll go to bat for you."

Harvey followed her lead as she pushed through the double doors into a huge storeroom full of steel shelves crammed with skids of boxes. Workers moved back and forth throughout the maze of shelves. Some were packing, others unloading goods with forklift trucks. Skylar took it all in within a matter of seconds.

Ahead of them in the first aisle was a man in a dark blue suit, clean cut, his hair trimmed to near perfection as was his large dark beard. He was wearing transparent glass frames and talking to one of the workers. He turned at the sound of Giles protesting.

"Giles?"

"Sorry, sir, I tried to stop them."

"Guessing you're William Akitt?" Harvey said.

He nodded.

"And you are?"

"Franklin County Sheriff's Department. We're here to inform you about the death of one of your investors. Ted Sampson."

"I already knew. It's unfortunate."

"You did? How so?"

"Word of mouth. News spreads fast in the town, Detective—?"

"Detective Baker," he said extending his hand and

shaking it. All the while Skylar remained quiet scoping out the activity and glancing up at the boxes. They all appeared to be unmarked. There was no sense of order unless of course they all contained the same thing.

"Oh, right, Nancy had mentioned you'd left messages. Sorry, it's been busy around here. Look, if you want to go speak with her, I'm sure she'll schedule you in."

"Schedule?" Harvey asked.

Skylar wandered down the aisle running her hands over boxes. "So what kind of products are you selling, Will?" She hopped up onto two pallets to get a better look inside.

"Can you not touch that, please?" he said waving with his arm and then telling Giles to deal with it. Skylar dug into a box and pulled out a load of packing filler. She had both arms inside emptying out Styrofoam noodles onto the floor until she latched on to something hard. She hauled out a white box that had an image of a phone on it.

"Cell phones? That's what your clients are buying?"

"Customized to work with our platform. Along with monetary wins, people can win all kinds of tech."

Giles put his hand out and she placed it in his hand and jumped down.

"You satisfied now, detective?"

"So why go to all this trouble selling or gifting products when you probably make enough money from the online gambling?"

"We like to think outside the box, detective. You can't just have your hands in one thing, you've got to be able to appeal to everyone. Those who sign up and spend fifty bucks get a free phone. We have incentives. Ways of getting people to become a member."

"What else you got in here?"

"Look, I haven't given you permission to go looking through this."

Skylar noticed that a number of the workers lugging boxes around were Latinos. None of them were wearing a uniform, just regular jeans, shirts and baseball caps. They eyed Skylar suspiciously. She'd assisted the ATF with numerous busts over the years, and she knew about the notorious Miami street gang referred to as the Latin Syndicate that had made a name for itself back in the '80s. They had their hands in everything from drug trafficking to illegal firearms to kidnapping, robbery and murder. They were bad news.

"You wouldn't mind if we interview a few of your employees, would you?"

Skylar brushed past Giles and headed towards a group of three that had been eyeing her since she'd come in.

"I have a good memory for faces, and I swear I've seen you before," she said pointing to one of them who began backing up. He got this wild look in his eyes and muttered something in Spanish and walked away from the group.

"Hey, where are you going?"

As she broke into a jog to catch up with him, he burst out of an emergency door.

"Harvey!" she shouted as she hurried after him at full sprint. As she shouldered the door, there was an eruption of gunfire and she darted back inside. Pulling her firearm, she tried again, this time she managed to get out without coming under heavy fire. A '93 Cadillac Fleetwood shot out of a row of vehicles, its engine roared and she ducked as several more rounds were squeezed off. Skylar hurried around the building with Harvey not far behind heading for his truck.

"Hold up, Skylar."

"I'm driving, toss me the keys."

"No you're not."

"You drive like the guy from *Driving Miss Daisy*."

"We've had this conversation before."

Harvey already looked out of breath by the time he made it around. She was sitting in the driver's seat with her hand out of the window waiting for him to toss the keys.

"Slide over."

"Just trust me."

He groaned and tossed her the keys. They were going to lose him if they didn't haul ass fast. Harvey barely had his second leg in the door when she tore away. Gravel kicked up the sides, spitting against the SUV like icy rain.

"Oh you've got to be kidding me. I just got this thing detailed."

She slammed her foot against the accelerator, crushing it to the metal, and careened out of the lot and onto Grays Avenue.

"You get one scratch on this and it's coming out of your paycheck."

"Ah you worry too much."

The Cadillac weaved its way around traffic heading east towards 12th Street. It took the turns so fast, the driver nearly lost control. Dirt and sand kicked up leaving a plume of dust in its wake. Harvey's SUV plowed through the dust and started closing the gap.

They were heading south towards US-98.

Harvey jumped on the radio to notify other police in the area.

"You've seen him before?" Harvey yelled over the roar of the engine.

"Two years ago, we were in Miami working with ATF to bring down two gangbangers selling illegal firearms. We busted down the doors on a few houses and flipped several of their buddies to find out where they were holing up. I swear, this guy was one of them."

"How the hell can you remember back that far?"

"They killed one of our task force members. A good friend of mine. How could I forget?"

The Cadillac must have reached a speed of ninety miles an hour. The driver swerved onto 98, not even slowing down to look for traffic heading in the opposite direction. Skylar had to slam on the brakes as a white truck trying to avoid the Cadillac lost control and mounted the shoulder plowing into a tree. Harvey called dispatch.

"We need EMT at the corner of 12th Street and 98."

Skylar tightened her grip on the wheel as the tires spun and shot forward heading after the guy. Fortunately there was a line of traffic on the road that day slowing everyone down. As they began closing the gap on the Cadillac it swerved into oncoming traffic causing every vehicle that was heading their way to pull over to the hard shoulder. Two vehicles lost control, hit a mound of dirt and flipped. Metal crunched and sparks flew as they slid across the ground.

"Skylar, let it go. Too many people are getting hurt."

"No. We need this guy."

"This is my vehicle. Now stop it."

She resisted for another minute then slammed the brakes on.

Harvey hopped out, and as soon as he slammed the door to walk around to the other side she took off leaving him in a cloud of sand and dust. There was no way in hell she was letting that guy get away after what he'd just done. She also didn't believe for one second that he was on the straight and narrow and holding down an honest job which raised the question of what kind of business was William Akitt running?

The two vehicles barreled down US-98 heading east. Trees whipped by in her peripheral vision. Between the branches she could make out water glistening. As she began gaining on him he started swerving from lane to lane to try and prevent her from coming up alongside. She was planning on doing a Pursuit Intervention Technique maneuver, which required getting the front of her vehicle in alignment with his rear tires and then smashing into the side of it causing it to spin out of control. Like road spikes, the PIT maneuver had pretty much become standard.

Problem was, he knew that too.

It wasn't the Latin Syndicate's first rodeo. Fleeing from the police was the norm, except they were used to the city. Skylar jerked the wheel to the left to make him think she was going that way and then in the next second, gunned the engine and slipped up the right of him. The Cadillac plowed into the side of Harv's SUV and sparks flew. She cast a glance in the side mirror and saw an excessive amount of paint damage. Oh, he was going to be pissed.

She had to stop this and soon. She jerked to the right,

then to the left and cracked the rear tires causing the back to slide and the front to turn. Skylar slammed her brakes on and watched as it spun out of control, slammed into a stop sign and flipped over on its side kicking dirt in the air. Glass smashed and metal crunched before there was an epic splash. She pulled the SUV over to the hard shoulder and hopped out, pulling her firearm and double-timing it over to the edge of the road. She pitched sideways and worked her way down.

The Cadillac was sinking into the water upside down.

Shit, she wanted the guy alive.

Within seconds she yanked off her jacket, tossed her weapon down and dived into the water. It took her breath away as she swam down to the side of the vehicle. Inside she could see he was already unconscious. She reached through the open window and unbuckled him, then dragged him out as the vehicle continued to sink down into a watery grave.

When she made it to the surface, she gasped for air. With her arm wrapped around him, she swam backwards to the shore. By that point, two uniformed officers were at the side of the road and so was Harvey.

She slumped down on the sandy shore gasping for air and spluttering while the officers took over.

"You pull a stunt like that again, and I will see to it the captain has your badge," Harvey yelled. "Besides, what the hell have you done to my SUV?"

"Good to see you too, partner," she said before spitting up water.

Chapter 8

Later that afternoon, Captain Davenport was fuming. As soon as they got back to the department, he hauled both of them in and had been pacing back and forth for a few minutes trying to find the words to convey his anger.

"Never in the history of this department have I seen such a screw-up. We have multiple accidents, two people in the hospital and a man dead. Now you want to explain to me how any of this has anything to do with Ted Sampson's death?"

"Skylar recognized the guy as being one of the Latin Syndicate."

Davenport eyed her with a look of death. "And that means?"

"It's rare you see these guys working 9 to 5 jobs, captain. I just wanted to question him but he decided to make a run for it."

"So we gave pursuit," Harvey said.

Skylar stabbed the air with her finger. "Actually, the accidents were caused by the guy driving his vehicle into oncoming traffic. He didn't need to do that."

"No, I will vouch for Skylar on that. He could have taken the hard shoulder but…"

"Oh, he also fired at me multiple times."

"That's true," Harvey said, nodding.

Skylar knew that Harvey didn't like the situation any more than Davenport did, but he knew that his head was on the chopping block as much as hers. If she went down, so did he as he'd been put in charge of keeping an eye on her and making sure her integration into the department went smoothly. This was anything but smooth.

"Okay but what I'm having a hard time understanding is why you were at Royal City to begin with?"

Skylar was quick to jump on that. "We spoke with Rachel Sampson and she'd mentioned that Ted had been investing money in a new startup. Our initial search of his personal computer showed email correspondence between him and the CEO William Akitt. So we headed over to speak to him."

"While at the same time notifying him about Ted's death."

Davenport waved his hand. "Hold on a minute. I was informed this was a suicide not a murder investigation."

"Well, it's not as simple as that," Skylar said, sticking her hand out to make a point.

"Actually I thought it was too but something doesn't add up about this one, captain. You see, the body was face up. Well I mean not exactly face up as he didn't have a head but you know what I mean. Body up and so forth."

Skylar was pleased to see Harvey acknowledging her expertise. She tapped his chest. "And don't forget his shoes were missing, and the socks were practically clean."

"Yeah, that's right," Harv said, his voice picking up speed in an attempt to get out as much as they could before Davenport ripped them a new one. He had a pinched expression which made it clear that he was not impressed by whatever they were telling him.

"Then of course there was the fact that he told his wife

he was working late but according to his medical assistant he left on time."

"Oh and then there was the home he was in the process of purchasing in Colorado."

Davenport threw up a hand, he'd heard enough. He didn't even need to say anything. He paced back and forth shaking his head. "This is a mess. I have a good mind to let Deputies Reznik and Hanson take this over."

"Come on, captain. We had no way of knowing he was going to take us on a high-speed chase."

"But you know protocol. If the risk of people getting hurt outweighs the need for the pursuit, you are to cease immediately. People were getting hurt. Didn't that register with you?"

"To be fair, captain, Harvey did want to stop the pursuit, and he got out. I was actually the one that continued."

"Thank you," Harvey said.

"Not a problem," Skylar replied.

"Would you two shut up? You're as bad as one

another. Harvey, you were meant to show her the ropes, not give them to her so she could hang herself."

"But—"

"No buts! Go home, both of you. I'm going to speak with Reznik, and the sheriff tomorrow, and figure out how to clean this mess up. It's going to be a PR disaster."

They exited his office and Skylar shook her head. Everything worked differently here compared to the U.S. Marshals. They followed protocol, but they always had a little more wiggle room for using their own discretion on what to do in dynamic situations that presented themselves. Of course she didn't expect the public to get hurt in the pursuit but at times that happened — it was par for the course in police work. They weren't the first cops to pursue an individual in a high-speed chase only to see it morph into a pile-up.

All eyes were on them when they entered the main office area. While Davenport had closed the blinds in his office, he didn't make a point of keeping his voice down. The entire department had heard the conversation.

Reznik and Hanson lounged in their seats with smirks on their faces. Hanson made a gun sign with his thumb and forefinger and winked at them. Of course to Skylar it didn't matter. She didn't give two hoots about office drama as she hadn't been there long enough. This was still her first day, and by the looks of it her last if Davenport had anything to say about it.

"Well it was bound to happen," Skylar said as she made her way out of the building into the parking lot.

"Bound to happen? Your reckless decision to continue to pursue him could have cost me my badge."

Skylar stopped and turned towards him. "And? You were looking at early retirement, anyway."

She turned away heading towards her truck.

"Who told you that?"

"Hanson and Reznik. They said you've lost your nerve."

"What? Lost my nerve?"

"I didn't say it. They did."

She continued on.

"Hey, wait up. Listen here. You've got it all wrong. When I retire, it's going to be on my terms not because of some adrenaline-fueled lunatic who's got a death wish."

"Everyone in this department has got a death wish, Harv, otherwise they wouldn't wear the badge and head out the door each day. None of us knows if we are coming home. And before you call bull crap on that, you tell me what your wife tells you before you leave each morning?"

He opened his mouth and then closed it.

"Exactly!" she said making her way over to the driver's side of her truck.

"Maybe that's so, but that doesn't mean I need to go out of my way to stick my neck out there. I've got a spouse and kids to think about. You don't!"

She stopped in her tracks and looked back at him. His words cut her to the core. "No, you're right. I don't, Harv." She placed her hand on the door handle getting ready to open it. "At the end of the day we're all responsible for our own choices. You make yours. I make mine."

She opened the truck door and slipped inside. She fired up the engine and brought the windows down to let in some of the breeze because the air conditioning unit had given up the ghost several weeks ago. Harvey placed a hand on the passenger side window.

"This is a partnership. Your decisions affect me, don't you get it? This isn't just about me not wanting to risk my ass, it's about me protecting yours. Or do you care so little about your own life that you're willing to throw it away?"

She shifted the gear into reverse and answered him without looking at him.

"Harv, I understand you've got my back, but you can't protect everyone and do this job. Eventually you are going to have to stick your neck out to get the job done, and maybe one day that means you don't get to come home. I'm willing to do that. If you're not, that's fine. It doesn't make you any less of a person. Retire, go play a round of golf, spend time with your wife and kids, cause it can all be swept away in a heartbeat. Trust me."

With that said she gunned the engine, and the truck tore back and she peeled out of the lot.

***

Skylar had no intention of going home. Her mind was still buzzing with the case. She figured if Davenport was going to reassign them the next day there wouldn't be any harm looking over Ted's truck that had been impounded so they could take inventory of any and all items found inside. An hour after getting herself a bite to eat, she headed over there. The sun was waning behind the trees as she pulled into the police impound. Depending on the size of the region, a department could have more than one impound.

Inside there were numerous vehicles that had been brought in for one reason or another. Some were related to accidents, others abandoned vehicles, and the rest were related to crimes.

She didn't plan on Deputy Hanson being there. He was chatting with a large guy who was in the process of driving a vehicle over to the far side of the lot.

"Hanson," Skylar said drawing up beside him. He cast a glance up and smiled.

"Heard you two were told to go home."

"And do what? Look, I just want to get a better idea of what they managed to find on the vehicle. Prints, hair samples and whatnot."

He groaned and shook his head. "The vehicle's been dusted and they have a number of prints and hair samples that have been sent over to the lab but it's going to take a while to get anything back. There were no tire tracks at the scene beyond Sampson's truck which feeds into the theory that he killed himself, however, there were a number of footprints which could mean that he was there to meet someone, and they arrived by skiff."

"And what about the cigarettes?"

"Reznik followed up with Rachel. He wasn't a smoker, so unless those belong to his assistant who does smoke by the way, possibly they were left by the killer — if he was killed. Right now we're still trying to establish that."

"What about his head? Did anyone find it?"

"We had divers out there today but nothing so far, it's very possible a gator took it. The boys will be back out again tomorrow, so maybe they'll come up lucky."

"Strikes me as a little odd there were no marks anywhere else on his body to indicate a gator had attacked him. You would think that he would at least have a few chunks taken out of him but nothing," Skylar replied. "Anyway, what are you doing here? I would have thought you and Reznik would be out there celebrating."

He smiled. "Contrary to what Harvey will tell you, we actually don't relish in his demise. We just haven't had the best relationship with him."

"How so?"

"A long story, maybe he'll tell you some time." He sniffed hard. "Anyway, I managed to take a cast of some of the footprints today and being as the soil out there was moist, I was looking to see if any of those prints matched what we found in the cab. Maybe if we can find a match that might feed into the theory that someone arrived by boat, perhaps had the conversation in the truck. It was raining that evening so it would make sense that if he was there to speak to someone that they sat in the vehicle."

She nodded. "So what items have you taken inventory of? Anything we missed?"

"The suicide note, the pack of Lucky Strikes, Jack Daniel's bottle and a Glock 22, which we have been able to confirm was registered in his name. All bullets were accounted for as well. But beyond that it's just your typical run-of-the-mill items. Gum, CDs, paperwork from oil changes and some loose change."

She scanned the truck, it was covered in fingerprint powder. Her mind churned over the conversation she'd had with Laura Jennings. The way she swatted her son around the head and the matter-of-fact way she spoke about her husband's death.

"Hanson, did you know Tucker Jennings?"

He tore off blue latex gloves and shifted his weight from one foot to the next. "Yeah, we had multiple run-ins with him in the past. Mostly domestics. Him and his old lady would get into it and we'd be out at their trailer separating them and whatnot. He drank like a fish. When he wasn't arguing with her, he'd find someone down at the local bar. He was a mechanic."

"And Lars Jackson?"

His eyebrows rose. "Cole Watson's cousin?"

"Cole Watson? The guy we busted at the convenience store?"

"Yeah, it's his cousin."

"Huh," Skylar said.

"Yeah, he doesn't have the best track record. He did time for theft eight years ago and has been pulled in a few times on drug possession but it was all minor stuff. Let's put it this way, he's bad news. Lars comes from a large family that has been living in these parts for the better part of two decades. They were involved in drug trafficking back in the '80s over in Everglades City. It was huge deal back in the '80s. Though now it's not so much marijuana as it is cocaine. Yeah, a number of them are doing time for it."

Hanson pulled out a pack of cigarettes and offered her one, she declined. He lit it and stood back from the vehicle admiring his handiwork. "It's just a matter of time, Skylar. One thing, there is always one thing that gets overlooked. I'm just hoping the lab results give us something." He took a hard drag on the cigarette. "You'll soon figure out how things work down here. I'm sure it's a big change from where you've come from. I'd always fancied joining the U.S. Marshals. Must have been a blast."

"It was," she said, her mind distracted by the connections she was making in her head based on what they'd discovered so far.

"So why did you leave?"

She snapped back into the present as his words caught up. "I hated New York winters."

He laughed, smoke coming out of his nostrils.

"Okay, thanks, Hanson. Let me know if you find anything else."

"Will do."

Chapter 9

The kitchen was full of steam. Payton was busy working away on her homework while Michael had his nose in his iPad. It was the first evening in a while they'd managed to get everyone together to eat around the table. With the way their schedules were, and the kids' sports activities in the evenings, they were usually grabbing up fast food or a snack on the way out the door. Elizabeth was taking out the roast chicken and potatoes when Harvey continued his rant. "I'm telling you, she's loco in a way that I can't even put into words but that's not the half of it, she has this way of flipping it back around and making you feel bad for saying anything," Harvey said, taking a huge gulp of his wine and then refilling his glass and going to refill hers. She put a hand over it.

"Steady there, I have to work tomorrow."

"At least you will have work. I have no clue what's going to happen tomorrow. Whether I'm going to get canned or promoted to errand boy. I swear, Elizabeth, this was not how I saw my return to the department. I mean, I've worked with other people before and trust me, Reznik and Hanson are one step away from the loony bin themselves but this woman, well, she redefines the term unstable."

She put her hand on his chest and smiled. "Harvey, you need to calm down. It's not going to do your stress levels any good. Perhaps she has a few personal problems. You've got to remember she comes from a fast-paced life in the city. I would imagine it would take anyone a while to become acclimated to Carrabelle. Anyway, how's the shoulder doing?"

He nodded. "I know." He rolled it a few times. "It's a little achy, though it could have been much worse. Perhaps a massage is in order."

She leaned into him. "I'll find out how much Barbara Ratlin charges."

He nearly spat out a mouthful of wine as she started laughing. "Dear God, please tell me that woman is not going to be here in the morning. I'm still aching from today's yoga session. You told me it was going to help. I feel in more pain now than I did after I was shot."

The doorbell rang and Payton shot off her seat to go and see who it was.

"Harvey, you're working muscles that you haven't used before. It's normal. It will eventually settle."

"Dad, it's for you," Payton said returning to the kitchen and taking her seat at the table. Harvey strolled down the corridor with a glass of wine in hand. He took a sip and chewed over what he was going to tell Barbara the next morning. That woman drove him up the wall. As soon as he opened the door he sighed. "C'mon," he said, stepping outside and looking up into the sky.

"What are you doing, Harv?" Skylar asked.

"Waiting for a bird to crap on me."

She made a confused expression. "Okay. Well, look, I just swung by as I was over at the impound, you know, looking to see what they had uncovered since taking Sampson's vehicle in."

"Oh, you were now. And was Davenport made aware of this?"

She scratched her forehead and continued without giving him his answer. "Anyway, Hanson didn't find any tire tracks at the scene besides Sampson's, but he did find a set of footprints that he's trying to match up with muddy prints in the truck. He figures if someone did meet him out there, that they chatted inside, because of the weather and all."

"Good to know."

"But it wasn't just that. Lars Jackson. Did you know his cousin is Cole Watson?"

"Of course I did, Skylar."

"And you don't see a connection?"

"Which would be?"

"You told me that Cole Watson had a lengthy rap sheet, right?"

He leaned against the doorway. "Right."

"We got Jackson's family who has known ties to drug trafficking helping the Jennings boy get his boat out there, and he's seeing Laura Jennings after her husband dies. So I did some digging around. Seems Ted Sampson was the one that dealt with the body of Tucker Jennings."

"Which of course he would because he was the medical examiner."

"What if Tucker Jennings's death wasn't an accident?"

Harvey stared back at her blankly as she shifted her weight looking a little uncomfortable.

"That's all interesting stuff, Skylar. Though I don't see the connection. Why not just take it to Reznik? As I'm pretty sure he'll be overseeing this case by tomorrow."

"That's tomorrow. This is today. And we don't know that for sure."

"After today, I'm pretty sure I know how this is going to play out."

"Listen, I'm sorry about the way things went today. I'll admit I overstepped the line, you're probably not used to driving in the fast lane."

"Oh because I'm not some big shot from the big city, well, I'll have you know—"

"Who is it, honey?" a voice called out from the back.

He turned. "Oh, it's nothing. I'll be with you in a sec."

Skylar smiled and shifted from one foot to the next. "Oh, um. Right. Sorry, did I interrupt?"

"We're about to have dinner."

"Okay, look, we can do this another time."

Right then Michael came to the door. He was a good-looking kid, about five six, dark hair styled with gel. He couldn't have been over seventeen. "Dad, mom said to have her come in and join us."

"Oh, I'm sure she has other things to do, don't you?"

Skylar's face lit up. "Actually, I was feeling a little hungry."

"You haven't eaten?"

"A sub but…"

"Harvey, c'mon, you're letting in all the heat, just bring her in, I want to meet her, anyway."

He grumbled under his breath.

Reluctantly he opened the door wide so she could come in. It was pointless trying to go against his wife, and once the kids clued in, he wouldn't have been able to live that down for a while. A new partner. Not inviting her in? He could already hear it.

Skylar smiled as she brushed past him. "You must be Michael?"

How did she know his name? He'd purposely not mentioned anything about his kids. His eyes narrowed. "Reznik!" That guy couldn't keep his mouth shut.

***

"Great place you have here," Skylar said looking around as Michael led her into the back where the kitchen was. It was a good-sized kitchen with a breakfast bar, and a large mahogany dining table that was already laid out with cutlery. As soon as she walked in, she caught sight of his youngest child and his wife, Elizabeth. She was a full-figured woman, big hair, not overly tall, reminded her a little of the celebrity chef Paula Deen, except twenty years younger. She just had that natural glow to her that made her seem personable.

"Welcome, welcome, Skylar." She greeted Skylar with

open arms and gave her a warm hug like she was meeting a long-lost relative. It seemed genuine, not forced and certainly not for show. She considered herself a pretty good judge of people and Elizabeth came off as if that was just her way.

"Michael, go grab the other chair."

He darted off and Skylar noticed their daughter. Dark hair, blue eyes, almost the spitting image of her mother. Looked to be around sixteen years of age.

"Come, take a load off your feet. Can I get you a drink?"

"That would be lovely, Mrs. Baker."

"Call me Elizabeth. Mrs. Baker seems so impersonal."

"Elizabeth it is."

Michael returned with a chair and she took a place. Over the course of the next twenty minutes they ate dinner, and Skylar felt a little awkward as if she'd invaded what should have been a private family time. Harvey scooped potatoes onto his plate and kept eyeing her like a store clerk who thought she was about to steal.

"So Harvey said you're living down at the marina, is that right?"

She was chewing away on a mouthful of food when she answered. "That's right. It's a catamaran. The boat belongs to a friend of mine."

"From the U.S. Marshals?"

She nodded.

Payton chimed in, nudging her brother. "I told you they let women become Marshals."

"So, that doesn't mean you are getting in."

"I can do whatever I like."

Harvey chimed in. "Your brother is right, Payton, it's not the life for you."

Skylar found that quite amusing. "And why would that be, Harv?"

"Well, you know, banging down doors, sticking your neck in the line of fire. It's…"

"Not for women?" She grinned turning her focus to Payton and addressing her directly. "You do know it's not all about apprehending fugitives. There's some pretty cool stuff you can do, such as transport federal prisoners, protect federal witnesses, seize assets and a lot more." She turned an eye towards Harvey. "You'd be surprised at how many women are Marshals."

"Yeah," Payton said. "See. It's not all about brawn, it's about brains."

Skylar winked at her.

"Still. I'd prefer if my daughter wasn't being endangered."

"Well, I'm sure she can make smart decisions."

Harvey cast a glance at his wife and then back at her. Skylar chewed her chicken.

"You know, this is really good. Best I've had in a long time, Elizabeth. Certainly beats microwave dinners and takeout."

She made a motion with her head as a sign of appreciation.

"Well, thank you, Skylar."

"Anyway, I think your dad has a good point, Payton. It can get a little hair-raising out there at times. There's certainly nothing like being shot at, or the buzz you get when you enter a building that you don't know is rigged with C4. It's quite a rush, actually."

Harvey's eyes widened.

She noticed and adjusted her tone a little. "I mean, if that's your thing. There certainly are safer lines of work available today."

Elizabeth got up and brought over dessert. It was an apple pie and ice cream. "Oh, I've got to say, Elizabeth, you have outdone yourself. I can now see why Harv is as slow as he is. I could get used to this."

"Probably best you skip it then," Harvey said, with a grin on his face.

"So Skylar, you have family living nearby?"

"My father lives in New York. Was a police detective for sixteen years. I haven't seen him in a while but he calls every now and again."

"And what about a special someone?" Elizabeth asked with a smile on her face.

She stopped eating and looked towards her, her

expression hardened. "I did, yeah. It didn't work out."

Harvey snorted but didn't say anything. She already figured he had his own preconceived views about her life. Whether they were accurate or not was neither here nor there.

"He died in an explosion six months ago."

Well, a pin could have been heard hitting the floor.

"I'm sorry to hear that, Skylar," Elizabeth said before glancing at Harvey who had paused with his fork an inch away from his mouth.

***

An hour later Skylar was about to leave and head down to the coroner's office by herself when Harvey told her to wait up while he fetched his jacket.

"You change your mind?"

"No but after what you said earlier. I kind of feel like an ass. I'm sorry. I didn't know about that. Why didn't you tell me?"

"Not exactly something you want to bring up when you first meet people. Hi, I'm Skylar, my fiancé was blown up in an explosion. Good to meet you."

He nodded. "Right. Let's go, we'll have to take your vehicle until mine is out of the body shop. I hope yours is working."

"Yeah, about that, I'll cover the cost."

"Of course you will," he said as he brushed past her.

It was pitch-dark out as they made their way through the town that night. Harvey kept shifting around trying to get comfortable. "Have you ever considered leasing or buying a second-hand vehicle?"

"I did. You're sitting in it."

"So tell me, why do you think there is some connection to Lars?"

"Look, it seems a little suspicious that you have people who are connected to known drug traffickers finding Ted's body. If they were involved in some way, it certainly would have given them time to plan it out, and so on."

"So you don't think Royal City has anything to do with it?"

"I didn't say that. I just find it a little suspicious. To be honest, I'm just trying to take it all in right now. I don't want to rule anything out. While we wait to hear back on the autopsy report and because we can't go banging on the doors of Royal City after today's incident, I figure we can at least look into a few things related to those who found him. I don't know about you, but I got a bad vibe from Laura Jennings."

"Because she hit her son? Get used to it, Skylar. I've seen that happen often around here."

"No, the way she spoke about her husband."

She parked in a spot and stepped out into the heat of the night. Thought it was slightly cooler, it was going to take some getting used to.

"You met the assistant before?"

"Nope," he replied pulling open a door and allowing her to go in first. They spent about five minutes in a waiting area until the woman appeared. Skylar took one look at Harvey's face and it said it all. She was a short woman sporting bright pink hair sticking up like a troll doll, except she was a pretty thing with fair skin. Early thirties, dark glasses, obviously had a thing for anything neon in color as her finger and toe nails were painted in bright yellow. She practically bounced her way over with a spring in her step. Harvey took one step back as she thrust her hand out.

"Detectives. Finally, we get to meet. I thought for a minute here I was going to have to solve this case all by myself. Jenna Madden."

"I'm Baker and this is Reid."

She shook their hands for an uncomfortable amount of time while smiling politely.

"So did you manage to dig out those records for Tucker Jennings?" Skylar asked.

"Yes, come this way," she led them away, walking at a pace that almost felt like a jog. "There wasn't a lot that I was able to unearth as his body is in the ground now but the file provides some details."

She led them into a small office.

"This was Sampson's."

"That it was. Unfortunately now it's mine."

"How long have you been working alongside him?"

"Eight months, give or take." She fished around in a cabinet and then pulled out a folder. "You'd think by now they would have all of this on a hard drive. Nope, we still have to keep a paper copy. Here we go," she handed it over and Skylar flipped it open.

"Well isn't that interesting?"

"What?" Harvey asked. Skylar handed it to him.

Chapter 10

The visit to the medical examiner's office had yielded some interesting findings from the death of Tucker Jennings. Skylar was gung-ho to speak with his wife, Laura, and Lars Jackson, but without the results of the autopsy on Ted, and details from the lab regarding prints in the truck, all they would have was general facts to go on. Jenna said she'd have the result of the autopsy to them by the following day so they turned in for the night.

When Skylar woke the next morning, she was still dressed in the same clothes from the previous day. She had once again fallen asleep in the U-shaped living area, though fortunately she was so tired when she got home, she didn't even need alcohol to fall asleep. The clock was flashing seven in the morning. Outside she could hear gulls screeching, and the gentle lapping of water against the boat. It had become almost therapeutic. Scot had told her that she could remain on the boat indefinitely as long as she could put up with him in the summer months when he would plan a visit. That suited her fine. She stumbled into the shower, pawing at her eyes and almost forgetting to take her clothes off.

She stubbed her toe on an empty bottle of Jack Daniel's on the floor and cursed before tossing it into a trash can. It clattered against three other empty bottles. She made a mental note to empty it later, a promise she'd made four times.

With one arm in a white shirt and doing up her pants with her other hand she reached over and took a bite of an apple before snatching up her phone to check her messages. She'd switched off the feature that caused it to buzz and noticed she'd already received two messages that morning.

One was from Hanson saying that they'd got a match on a footprint found in the truck to one leading to and from the swamp. However without Ted's shoes, they were unable to tell if they belonged to someone else as only one print was lifted from the truck. The other was from

Harvey asking her to call him when she was awake.

She tapped in his number and brought the phone up to her ear as she continued getting ready for work. Her mind was buzzing and felt like a New York freeway. She couldn't stop thinking about those who'd been injured yesterday, along with the death of the Latin Syndicate member. She knew she wasn't at fault for the injuries, as the man they'd identified as Tito Martinez had caused the accidents, but she couldn't help feel responsible for whatever the captain was going to decide today. For all she knew, they might get placed on administrative duty, or reassigned to some godforsaken division in the department doing some duty that no one else wanted.

"Skylar, do you not answer your phone or are you just ignoring me?" Harvey said.

"I must have switched off the ringer last night. Anyway, what's up?"

"Axl was in contact with me last night, he managed to get into Ted's laptop, and unearthed some details about a separate account, as well as two online payment processing accounts he was using to shift money around. Anyway, last night I headed down to the station after we parted ways and spent some time going over Ted's financial records. On the surface everything seems normal, however when taking into account the online payment processor which he also used for gambling, we find quite an operation. It appears he opened an offshore bank account in the Cayman Islands around the time he began investing in Royal City. Here's the thing. His regular account that is in his and Rachel's name seems to show signs that he was spending more than he was making, however the account in the Caymans was racking up some serious money. There were a lot of big deposits within a matter of two months. I'm talking in the hundreds of thousands. There were also some big withdrawals. The interesting part is that he was transferring money as and when needed from the Caymans account into one of the two payment processor accounts, then he'd transfer it to a second, and then it would go into another bank account that is not listed as the same one he was receiving his paychecks into or sharing with Rachel, hence the reason why she wouldn't have batted an eye about the finances. It really doesn't make sense unless he was wanting to avoid paying taxes then I can see why he had that offshore account but why shift all that money around? Anyway, I'm trying to get in contact with the second bank about that account here in Florida and we might have to subpoena them in order to get more details. Either way it raises a lot of questions about his connection with Royal City as the stream of money being paid to him came from them. What he was doing with it is another thing entirely but I'd be interested to know what the deal is there. Was it gambling winnings? Interest from Royal City?"

Skylar nodded thoughtfully. "What I find interesting is that he was willing to risk a large sum of money by investing in an early stage, pre-profitable company. That's risky as an investor. We know that most start-up companies fail. Without knowing if it's going to be a home run, why would anyone do it?"

"It had to have offered the possibility of a home run. He must have figured he could get a return of 10, 20 maybe 30 times more otherwise I doubt he would have risked it. I mean going by his financial records he had some savings but based on the way he was spending money, to risk those savings would have been crazy."

"Certainly explains how he could make the purchase of another home before selling the one he had," she said.

Silence stretched between them.

"Anyway, Jenna will have the autopsy results this morning. Toxicology will take longer but at least we will be able to know a little more about how he died and the time of death. From there I think we should have a little chat with Laura Jennings and then track down Lars," Harvey said.

"You heard from Davenport yet?" Skylar asked.

"No so far. No news is good news in my books."

"Well I'll meet you in, half an hour? I got to find me some coffee, get my head out of this fog and—"

"So when are you going to show me this boat?"

"You can come down to the Moorings anytime you like."

"I might just do that. See you in thirty," he said before hanging up.

Skylar ventured out onto the deck and took in the sight of the overcast sky. Overnight storm clouds had formed, threatening more rain. She grumbled and observed a boat slowly coming into a slip beside her. At the helm was an old-timer, white beard, a black-and-white skull bandana around his head. He spotted her and made a friendly gesture by saluting.

"Good morning."

"That's still to be determined," she replied hopping off and giving a short wave. That was her usual reply whether things were going well or not. It had always struck her as a strange gesture to make. It implied that the morning was good but for who? And what was a bad morning? Once again, her mind overanalyzed. In the few months she'd been down at the Moorings she hadn't taken the time to drop in on a small café beside the hotel that was often used by folks not wishing to sleep on their boat. It was called Vagabond. It had only recently opened up and being as she was out of coffee, she decided to give it a whirl.

A cluster of boat owners huddled around outside drinking coffee and sitting at patio tables. There was a steady influx. Skylar glanced at a blackboard A-frame that listed the special brew of the day. *Dog Island Roast: This nutty artisanal coffee has an intense flavor that will explode in your mouth. Powerful enough to wake Odin from his sleep, you can be sure its bold flavor will put the bark in your day!* Jeesh, who came up with these lines? Dog Island Roast? She chuckled as she stepped inside the small café. A bell over the door let out a shrill and a small Chinese guy behind the counter yelled like a foghorn, "How are you? Welcome to Vagabond."

If the coffee wasn't good, his voice would have woken her up. It was beyond startling. For a second she thought that maybe she was the only one he did it to until two more people came in after her. He repeated the phrase, each time with a big smile on his face as he fluttered around behind the counter like Tom Cruise in *Cocktail.* He was tossing up bottles of flavoring, hitting the buttons on café machines and taking cash all at the same time. The guy was a one-man army and by the looks of it, able to keep everyone happy. The place had a hip look, except it carried a dockside theme. It had a bow-shaped bar and rigging ropes along the walls with mirrors that were meant to look like ports. The aroma of coffee attacked her senses, snapping her awake as she got in line behind an old couple who were obviously from out of town as between placing their order they were arguing over what they were going to do that day.

When she made it to the front of the line, the guy was still beaming. She would have been sweating up a storm after the number of folks he'd just served. He was a short guy, maybe five foot five and reminded her of Jet Li. Early fifties, a few crow's feet around his eyes. His entire outfit that morning was black, tight and gave her the impression that he'd left his ninja mask at home. She noticed his nametag had the name Donnie Wu engraved into the gold plate.

"Ah, you're the new detective, right?"

"Oh, news travels fast." She cast her eyes over the pastries he had to offer.

"It does when your mug shot is on the front of a newspaper."

He reached underneath and tossed down *The Apalachicola Times*. Sure enough there was a snapshot of her soaking wet standing beside several cruisers as they dragged Tito's vehicle out of the bay. She ran a hand over her face and groaned. This was not good. She immediately envisioned Davenport unfolding the paper and spitting his morning glass of orange juice all over the table. Though it was troubling to her, apparently not to Donnie.

"What can I get you? The first one is on the house."

Although his ancestry was Chinese, his American English was perfect.

"Really? That's kind of you."

"Ah, it's the first bit of action we've seen in these parts in a while."

She tried to shift the topic away from yesterday's incident.

"What do you recommend?"

"That depends how you take your coffee?"

"Well that depends on how fresh yesterday's grinds are."

His faced contorted, a look of horror. "Please tell me you are joking."

"I wish I was."

He raised a finger. "That has to stop. From now on you will come here every morning."

"Oh I don't know about that. It can get pretty costly and well, the department doesn't pay much."

"I insist. Nothing grinds my gears more than to hear that people are accepting less than stellar coffee in the morning."

"Okay, point taken," she said. "I'll take a cup of your Dog's Island."

"Great choice."

He went about making it while she stepped to one side and cast her gaze around the room. "So this a new venture for you, Donnie? What did you do before this?"

"I ran a brothel."

Her eyes widened. He started laughing. "I'm kidding, I was in information technology in Utah. My wife and I used to come here for the winters, she always wanted to open up a café so here we are."

"Nice." Skylar looked around. "So where is Mrs. Wu?"

"Salt Lake City Cemetery. One year ago."

"Oh, I'm sorry."

He was in the middle of making her drink when he stopped and turned around. "There is a saying. When the winds of change blow, some people build walls and others build windmills." He stood there for a second contemplating it before continuing on. Something about what he said affected her. She felt a lump form in her throat. He didn't try to explain it, neither did he ask for her to not pity him, he simply smiled and went about completing her coffee. She however was struck by his positive attitude. Even as he turned, and she handed him payment, she couldn't help think about how it applied to her situation.

She backed up so the next person could be served.

"Thanks, Donnie."

"Not a problem. You be sure to show up tomorrow." His face winced. "No more drinking coffee from yesterday's grinds." She nodded. Even what he said there made her think. It was like a proverb in itself. He gave a wave and returned to serving the next customer with as much enthusiasm as he had her.

***

Harvey was waiting for her outside the Franklin County M.E.'s office. It looked a lot different in the day than at night. It was modern looking, with palm trees either side of the walkway and pristine landscaping that would make anyone turn their head twice. She was running about ten minutes late. He was leaned up against a new vehicle, a silver Ford Edge. She parked her exhaust-polluting heap of crap beside his and hopped out.

"Decide to trade in your other?"

"It's a rental until I get my vehicle back, and no, you are not driving this." He paused. "What took you so long?"

She sipped on her coffee. "Sorry. I got caught up at Vagabond."

"Oh that new café. What's that like?" he said coming around and falling in step as they approached the coroner's office.

"Insightful," Skylar replied.

"Heard there is some foreigner running it."

"The guy's American."

He tossed up his hands. "Oh, I'm not racist. I was just pointing out what I'd heard."

"Well maybe they should talk to the guy. Man, people's perceptions are skewed."

She pulled open the door, and they went inside. Five minutes later they were standing in a sterile-looking room that served as the autopsy room. It had a tiled floor and several examination tables that were empty. They were surrounded by stainless-steel refrigeration compartment doors. Jenna pulled out the body of Ted Sampson. He was covered by a white sheet and had a tag on his discolored toe.

"The autopsy only took a couple of hours and I can give you the preliminary results now but the best results will come later. I know you were hoping to get that toxicology report back sooner, and the official report will come back in four to six weeks, so I did up my own test which should at least provide you some insights into answering the question about blood alcohol levels which are usually available for up to forty-eight hours. What I was able to do was collect peritoneal cavity blood, along with urine, and run a couple of tests. Now again, don't quote me on this as you would have to wait for the lab results, but based on my findings it appears that he was alcohol-free at the time of death. However his blood alcohol levels were high. Now this can happen because a high glucose concentration and bacteria in postmortem blood can produce alcohol as the sugar gets converted to alcohol, which causes a high blood alcohol level. So that's why I had to analyze the urine, which showed zero for alcohol, N-propanol and acetaldehyde."

"In English, Jenna," Skylar said.

"I'm just saying I'm pretty certain that when we get back those results from the lab, they are going to say that he didn't have any alcohol in his body at the time of death, however, there was alcohol in his body after. Meaning it's my belief based on the findings that he died and then had alcohol poured into his body. Similar to the Tucker Jennings case, however, his toxicology report listed that he had traces of alcohol in his system prior to death but not enough that it would have impaired him. The high level in his system was found after death. All in all, Ted's death and Tucker's are similar in the way they were found dead. They only vary in alcohol levels."

"That's like ballistics matching up one bullet from one gun being used in the death of someone else," Harvey said.

"Somewhat," Jenna replied. "What is confusing is why Ted marked Tucker's cause of death as inconclusive."

"Okay, so we understand what happened to Tucker, but what about Ted's cause of death?"

"While we don't have his head, based on my testing I found a few ligature marks around his neck, and in the groin area it showed housefly larvae which means they had to have been laid on his body indoors and under warm conditions. In other words Ted Sampson was dead before he hit the water. He died sometime between ten and midnight. Based on the findings, he was strangled to death, which would explain why no blood was found at the scene."

"There we go," Skylar said. "So the truck was staged. That proves that someone was involved in the disposal of his body into the water and also gives credence to why he was face up as he didn't drown and why his socks weren't heavily soaked in soil. Someone killed him somewhere else, poured alcohol into his body, drove him there and then dumped him into the water and left via the water.

Whether his head is found by the diving team, it doesn't matter. The proof is in the autopsy. Good job, Jenna. Now we just need to know who was behind it and what the motive was."

Skylar turned to head out.

"Where are you going?"

"To find Lars Jackson."

Harvey nodded. "I'll go speak with William Akitt, find out what was going on with the money that was being paid out to Ted."

Chapter 11

After getting the address from Hanson for Jackson, she headed along US-98 towards Eastpoint. It was an easy twenty-minute drive along the coast. The town was located across from St. George Island and Apalachicola. Similar in size to Carrabelle, it was considered the nose of the Forgotten Coast. A thriving community full of shrimp and oyster boats, it represented another slice of Florida that was practically untouched by tourist traps. It came as no surprise to her to discover that Lars Jackson owned a fishing charter called Jackson's River Fishing and Sightseeing Tours. It operated out of a warehouse just off US-98 at the corner of 2nd Street. Skylar veered into a parking spot. There were several Chevy and GMC trucks outside with his logo of a fishing reel and anchor on the side. As she got out, several yellow flies made their way in nipping at her flesh. She swatted them away and headed into the main office. A middle-aged Hispanic woman was the receptionist. She was smoking a cigarette and had a large coffee beside her. Her desk was covered in paperwork, a real disorganized mess. The whole inside of the building reeked of smoke and the ceilings were yellow from nicotine.

"Morning, I'm from the Franklin County Sheriff's Department, would Lars Jackson be around?"

She squinted, looking her up and down. "I believe he's out back, I'll go check. If you want to take a seat, I'll be right back."

Skylar turned her attention to a cabinet full of awards and photos of Little League teams the company supported. For someone that was supposed to have a history of drug trafficking, either he was hiding his soft side or all of that was just a front. It wouldn't have been the first time she'd seen companies involved in drug and gun running operating a business that looked legit to cover for their illegal activities.

The woman returned. "Come right this way," she said

lifting up a section of the counter to let her into the back. She followed her down a dimly lit corridor that was packed with boxes of paperwork and folders. Her eyes drifted over photos in frames that provided aerial shots of the East Bay, Apalachicola Bay and the Gulf. Most were images of fishing trips.

Led into the back of the warehouse, she saw a number of boats up on wooden blocks and trailers. Several guys who were hard at work painting the bow of a boat looked over at her and scanned her like a bar code. Nothing about guys ogling her made her feel uncomfortable. In her line of work, she was used to the long stares and men questioning her ability to do the job.

The woman made a motion with her hand towards a man that was slid under a truck. He was dressed in blue overalls and all that was sticking out was his legs.

"Lars Jackson."

"That would be me."

He was laying on a red padded bench with rollers. He slid out from underneath the truck and squinted. Lars had to be in his mid-thirties, bulky guy, a full head of hair that was long and swept back into a ponytail. He had really bad stubble. The kind that looked like he'd tried to trim it and had missed areas.

She flashed her badge. "Need to talk to you about Tucker Jennings."

"I told the police everything I knew back when it happened. It's in the report."

He slid back under. She reached down and grabbed a hold of the end and tugged it out causing him to slide back into view. This time she put her foot on the edge of it to prevent him from doing it again.

"You want to refresh my memory?"

He sighed and took out a rag as he got up and wiped his hands off. "Not much to tell you. He worked here as a mechanic on the boats part-time, and on vehicles in Carrabelle the rest of the time. That's how I knew him."

"Is that how you got to know his wife?"

Lars eyed her as he made his way over to a sink. He dipped his hand in Fast Orange Hand Cleaner, rubbed it around his hands and washed them under water. "I knew Laura long before she hooked up with Tucker. We used to date way back in the day but parted ways. We remained friends. She came to me when he was knocking her around. You know, getting drunk and taking it out on her and the kid."

"So, what, you stepped in?"

He dried off his hands on a dirty white towel. "I spoke with him, told him he needed to sort himself out or he could find another job."

"So you were his boss."

He leaned back against the counter and stared at her.

"You're new around here, aren't you?"

She didn't answer him but pressed for more details. "How long did he work for you?"

She smirked when he didn't reply.

"Four years," he finally said. He tossed the towel down and walked over to a wooden bench and snatched up a pack of smokes. He tapped one out. "Never missed a day of work. Generally, a good worker unless he'd been drinking."

"You ever go fishing with him?"

He lit the cigarette and blew out a plume of smoke near her face.

"You mean, did he ever go fishing with me? I was the one that got him into it. If it wasn't for me, he would have spent most of his days down at the local bar. For the sake of Laura, I tried to get him to go out with me fishing. See if I could get him to think straight. You know, befriend him."

"That's admirable. You do that with all your employees or only the ones whose wives you plan on bedding?"

He smiled and wagged his finger in front of her face. "You know, Detective..."

"Reid."

"Reid. My family has deep roots in these parts — connections that have been made over the years. I would hate to see a lovely woman like yourself affected by accusations."

"Oh I think I can take care of myself."

"I bet you can." He looked her up and down like a hunk of meat. "Listen up, I didn't start seeing Laura until after Tucker was in the ground. We reconnected over the funeral. I told her I would take her kid out from time to time. So before you start insinuating that I was having an affair while she was with Tucker, think again."

She nodded. "Where were you between ten and midnight two nights ago?"

He took a hard drag on his cigarette. "Doing a spot of night fishing."

"Down at Otter Creek Swamp?"

"No, it was work related here in the Gulf."

"But you gave Ricky Jennings a hand getting a boat into the swamp the next morning?"

"I did. Is there a law against that?"

"Can anyone confirm your alibi from two nights ago?"

"Only those I work with."

"You mean, those you employ?"

"If you're splitting hairs. You can check the records

out front. I was here."

She stared at him and his eyes shifted. "You ever meet Ted Sampson?"

"Who?"

"Ted Sampson."

He shook his head. "Not familiar with that name."

Lars dropped the remainder of his cigarette to the ground and crushed it below his boot. "Look, I've got a lot of work to be done so if you don't mind."

"So you mostly do tours here?"

He sighed. "That and we charter boats for groups of folks who want to do some fishing. It's honest work."

"I imagine it is. If that's all you're doing."

He turned back to her as he was heading towards the truck. "What do you mean by that?"

"I might be new around here but I've heard of the reputation that your family has got with drug trafficking."

"That was a long time ago."

"Maybe but your rap sheet has you in possession of drugs not that long ago."

"I did my time, and that was minor stuff. Now unless there is anything else, I've got to get back to work."

She nodded and broke away from him. "I'll go get those records you mentioned."

"You do that," he said eyeing her. She could feel his eyes boring into her back as she walked away. She had a sense that he wasn't being forthright about something but whether that was related to Tucker's or Ted's death was to be seen.

***

"I told you. I was not aware of his ties to the Latin Syndicate," William Akitt said. He looked uncomfortable sitting behind his stylish desk in an oversized office which gave him a stunning view of the bay.

"So you're just in the habit of hiring anyone without background checks?"

He leaned forward. "Detective, we run a busy house here. I'm not involved in the hiring or firing, that is down to Giles."

"And yet you oversee products being sold and

investors?"

He scowled back at him. "Your point?"

"My point is that within a matter of weeks of Ted stepping forward as an investor, large sums of money wound up in his account, all of which are coming from Royal City."

"Your friend was a gambler, detective. In fact he was one of our best clients as well as being an investor. He took funds he won through our website and reinvested them so any deposits or withdrawals you are seeing, are probably related to that."

He reached for a glass of water and took a sip. Harvey never took his eyes off him for even a second. "Well, I might be able to buy that, however, his records indicate he was using your service for months prior to when the assumed winnings entered his account. His string of luck wasn't as good back then, but the moment he becomes an investor, I'm expected to believe he had the luck of the Irish?"

"I'm not sure what you're wanting from me? We have

a number of investors and many of those are clients who gamble. The reason they are investing is because they have seen the potential of what we are doing here. Growth has been off the charts in the first quarter of business so it's no surprise that you're seeing large sums of money being transferred. Our business is an open book, detective. We have nothing to hide. I feel for Ted's wife and son but there isn't much I can do to help you. I've already told you that on the night of his death, I was in Miami having meetings with potential investors. I've already provided your department with the details of that and they have cleared me."

"Be assured, Mr. Akitt. If it comes to our attention that you have been hindering a police investigation by not being honest, this won't end well for you or Royal City."

"Like I said, detective, investigate away, we have nothing to hide."

He smiled and Harvey got a sense that he thought he was above the law, that just because his lawyers had come down heavy on the department over the recent events regarding Tito, he thought he was untouchable.

"I'm going to need the names of those investors so I can follow up with them. You know, just to verify you were where you said you were," Harvey replied. William didn't seem to bat an eye. He turned around and fished into a drawer and then handed over a list of names with phone numbers and addresses. He took a pen and circled the ones that he had been with that night. Harvey thanked him for his time, then got up and told him he would let himself out.

Outside in the parking lot he beat a hand against his vehicle. They were so close but something was still missing. Ted was a good friend, and regardless of what he'd got himself caught up in, he wasn't going to let this slide until he saw whoever had killed him in handcuffs.

Chapter 12

It was a little after eleven that morning when Davenport pulled them both back into his office. Skylar eyed Harvey and even though they were both involved in the incident on US-98, she was the one that had performed the PIT maneuver so if anyone was going down, it would be her.

"Captain, I just want to be the first to say that I don't think Harvey should be held responsible for anything that occurred yesterday. He was basically following my lead. If you are going to place me on paid admin leave, then so be it."

"Settle down. Your partner has already gone to bat for you. I've given a lot of thought to this and discussed it with Sheriff Sloan. Fortunately, we were able to pull video footage from Harvey's dashcam. That has allowed us to verify what happened. You're not at fault for the accidents of civilians and thankfully none of them died. You were right to perform the PIT maneuver before any additional lives were placed in jeopardy. Now, Harvey has explained that there has been a development in the case with the autopsy report and that this is now being treated as a homicide." He paused taking a sip of his coffee. "I'm not going to reassign you. Though when I tell you to go home, I mean go home and don't work on the case," he said with a smirk on his face. "However, don't be surprised if a civil lawsuit is filed against you because of the death of Tito. I expect his family will want answers even though we have been able to verify that there was a warrant out for his arrest at the time that you tried to question him. I don't believe you will be held at fault because you were performing your duties. I'll be speaking with the state attorney general to see how we can get this smoothed out. In the meantime I want you two to get back to work. That's it!" he said going back around his desk and taking a seat.

Both of them stood there.

"Well go on. Get out of my office before I change my

mind."

"Yes sir."

They backed out, and she closed the door behind them.

"You spoke on my behalf?"

Harvey smiled and kept walking.

"Harvey."

"Before you get all sentimental. They requested my dashcam. I handed it over. I didn't go to bat. Heck, I wanted to take a bat to you and knock some sense into you. You still owe me for that. The paint job is pricey too."

She stood there with a smile.

"Anyway, how did you get on with Jackson?"

She moved ahead, and they ventured out of the office. The sun had started to come out, and the atmosphere had thickened. A warm breeze blew against her cheeks as they headed over to her truck.

"Ah, he says he was fishing that night. I pulled up the records from the front desk but that doesn't confirm anything. As he's the boss of his company, of course his employees aren't going to say anything. I couldn't get anything out of them beside a grunt or an eye roll. They certainly don't like cops."

Harvey laughed. "Welcome to Franklin County. The Jacksons have deep roots in these parts."

"That's what he said."

Harvey hopped in the passenger seat.

"You want to fill me in on that?"

"I will on the way."

"To where?"

"We're going to pay Cole Watson a little visit. Loyalty is big in these parts, Reid, but when your neck is on the chopping block, you'd be surprised at who they'd throw under the bus to get a better plea deal."

As they pulled out and made their way towards Franklin County Correctional Institution located on FL-67 north, Skylar brought the windows down.

"Seriously, you need to spend your first paycheck on getting the air conditioning fixed in this."

"We could have taken your rental."

"Yeah, look at what happened to my SUV. That's not happening. Nope, from now on we either take a cruiser or your vehicle."

She reached over and snatched up some gum and offered him a stick. He declined.

"So what's the scoop on the Jacksons? I already know their family was involved in drug trafficking. So are they all bottom-feeding crooks?"

He chuckled. "No, that's just their offspring. Callum Jackson is the brains behind the organization. That man is untouchable. At least no one yet has been able to pin anything on him. He hides behind a wall of lawyers and lives in a number of beachfront mansions. One on St. George Island, another in Apalachicola and another in Eastpoint. He has his fingers in a little of everything; real estate, charter business and used vehicles. You name a business and he's pulling the strings behind it somewhere. Several years ago there was a big sting operation similar to the one they did back in the '80s in Everglades City. We were involved along with a number of police departments. It was a joint effort. Well, somehow even though his name got dropped by several of the people that were arrested, no one was able to pin anything on him. There was just no evidence. So he gets to live a free man for another day. But here's the thing. His family, they are at the bottom of the rung. They've all been in and out of prison for one reason or another. Now we keep a close eye on their business ventures."

"Obviously not close enough," Skylar said shooting him a sideways glance.

"It's all about patience down here, Reid. This isn't the big city where you can get away with a lot. They make sure we dot our I's and cross our T's down here. You'll soon get the hang of it."

"Oh so you see hope for me, do you?"

He laughed. "By the way, before we head over to county, stop off at Carrabelle Junction. I'm feeling hungry and I could use the caffeine."

"Why not grab something from—"

"Vagabond?" He paused. "Loyalty is big around here, Reid. You can't be just switching cafés. Besides, Barbara does my coffee just right. You'll see."

Skylar veered into a parking spot outside the low-slung yellow building with a blue roof. Along the top the sign listed what they offered: espresso, sandwiches, soups, salads and ice cream. They hopped out and several people coming out of the café said hello to Harvey.

"Quite a star around here," Skylar said.

"Work long enough in this town, you'll see the same faces. It's a tight-knit community. Come on, I'll introduce you to Barb, she'll be horrified when I tell her where you get your coffee."

Stepping inside was like stepping back in time. It had a '50s theme to it. Black-and-white checkered floor, red seating and lots of vintage signage all over the walls from the '50s and '60s. She saw a sign that said: Real Food for Real People. There was even a fake palm tree inside.

"Detective Baker."

A woman behind the counter who looked like Cyndi

Lauper was all glammed up with huge hoop earrings and a bright red apron. She had a big grin on her face as she collected cash from someone before turning her attention to Harvey. She leaned forward across the counter flashing her huge cleavage.

"So darling, what can I get you?"

"The usual."

"And for your friend here?"

"Barb, this is Skylar Reid. My new partner."

She burst into laughter. "A partner? For you?"

He shook his head and both of them glanced at her like she was some lab rat. "I know, I told them the same thing but Davenport wouldn't listen."

"Haven't seen him in here for a while."

"Oh he's probably going to the other café. The same one Skylar frequents."

"I only went once."

"Once is too many, ain't that right, Barb?"

Her mouth pursed tight, and she squinted. "Hon, once you taste my coffee, you won't be heading back to

Mr. Miyagi's store."

"I believe Miyagi was Japanese, not Chinese," Skylar shot back.

She roared with laughter. "Oh, we've got a live one here. Your work is cut out for you, Harv. Does she correct your grammar too?" She smiled and then leaned across and touched her arm. "I'm just ribbing you, darlin'. What can I get you?"

"Espresso sounds good."

"Coming right up."

Harvey was still trying to settle himself from laughing so much. He sat on a stool and swiveled around so he could take in the view.

"You really think Cole has anything to say?"

"With a charge of attempted armed robbery, I doubt we will be able to get his gums to stop flapping. For all we know he could have been the one responsible. He was out when Ted was murdered. He's been on Callum's payroll since he got out of jail. That's the thing about Callum Jackson, Reid. He would go to any extent to line his pockets."

Barb returned with their drinks, Harvey tossed down a couple of bills and thanked her and they headed out. He bit into a ham and swiss croissant and he continued talking about Callum.

"You'll see him, eventually. Once Callum catches wind that there is new blood in the department he will be along to invite you out to one of his mansions. He's done it with everyone."

"Bribing?"

"Oh no, he's very careful about how he attempts to bribe members of the department cause he doesn't know you. No, it's just his way of testing the waters, feeling you out and seeing if he can trust you. He usually invites you out under the guise that he might have some off-duty security work that pays well."

"Right, yeah, that's common."

"Some of these guys work their shift, Skylar, and if they can earn extra outside with private paid duty, it allows them to fatten their wallet. You can't fault them for doing it. Not everyone earns the big money like we do," he said grinning before he took another bite of his food and crumbs went all over the floor of the truck.

"Hey, use a napkin."

"Skylar, there are four empty coffee cups rolling around on the floor, a half-eaten apple and what appears to be gum stuck to this seat. And you're complaining about a few crumbs."

"I run a tight ship," she replied with a smile.

"Then I would hate to see your boat."

"Oh you will. All in good time."

They drove in silence for ten minutes while Harvey followed up with several of the investors that had been in talks with William on the night Ted was murdered. After getting off the phone he sighed.

"Seems like his alibi is solid. I ran checks with the hotel where he'd met them in Miami and there is a record of him paying with his credit card and the hotel had him on their camera system."

"Well I wouldn't expect he would be the man behind

it, anyway. He might be running a business that is a little shady, but he seems like the kind of guy who would have paid someone to kill Ted. The question still remains, though, why?"

"I'm having Hanson follow up with the payment processors today and check into that third bank account. It's a very odd system he had. He was getting money from Royal City, it was going into one PayPal account, then he was taking some of that money and transferring it into his offshore account and also placing some in a second PayPal account that was linked up to another bank account here in Franklin County. So he had two online payment processors and what appears to be three bank accounts: his regular shared account with Rachel, the offshore one and the other one."

The Franklin Correctional Institution was set back from FL-67. It looked like a FEMA camp with one-story buildings and chain-link fence wrapped around it covered by barbed wire. She drove up the long driveway that took them up to the gates. Harvey had already made the arrangements earlier that morning to see him so as soon as they arrived, he flashed his badge and they were let inside the inner gates. According to Harvey, the state prison had come under scrutiny in recent months after a disturbing number of cases involving inmates that had died after being beaten by guards.

After parking, they headed over to a security gate.

They were met by a prison guard who took them through a series of heavy barred doors before they were brought into what they were told was used for interviews with inmates. There was not much to it. No camera inside. Just a table and four chairs.

They waited in there for close to five minutes before Cole Watson was brought in. He was dressed in the typical blue prison garb, white sneakers and white T-shirt. He scowled immediately when he saw them, and his eyes opened wide when he laid eyes on Skylar.

"Oh no!"

"Just take a seat, we're just here to talk."

"I want the guard staying in the room. I know how

you cops work. Police brutality and all."

"How's the finger?" Skylar asked.

He cursed at her and she smiled. Cole Watson's eyes were sunken, and his teeth were a mess — all the consequences of taking meth. These kinds of guys didn't learn. Their teeth could fall out and their skin would show signs of falling apart and they would still keep taking drugs. It was sad really.

"Shouldn't I have a lawyer?"

"We can get you one but I don't think you'll need it," Harvey said. "Besides, it just slows down the process."

"What process?"

Harvey cast a glance at Skylar. "Can we get you a coffee, a cigarette?"

Cole snickered. "Oh I see how it is. First you put me away and now you want to befriend me?"

"Okay, we'll continue without."

"No. No. I'll take the cigarette."

Harvey reached into his pocket and pulled out a pack that hadn't been unwrapped. He tore the clear plastic off and tapped one out. Cole leaned forward. His eyes were on Skylar as he took the cigarette between his lips and then Harvey lit it. He let him get the nicotine into his system before he continued with any questions.

"So Cole. Does the name Ted Sampson ring a bell?"

He adjusted in his seat, the cuffs clanging against the table. "Nope."

"Where were you two nights ago between the time of ten and midnight?"

He took a hard pull on his cigarette and squinted as gray smoke curled up into his eye.

"I was at home. I had a few brews."

"You worked for Lars Jackson, isn't that right?" Skylar interjected.

Through slit eyes he answered, "And?"

"You were not out with him that night, fishing?"

He pulled a face. "Nope. Like I said, I went to the bar that night. Marine Street Grill. Then I got home around ten and watched a rerun of *Law and Order*, cause you know how much I love me some good old detective work." He grinned flashing his black teeth.

"Can anyone verify that?"

"Check with Marine Street Grill."

"Well that's only going to let us know that you went to the bar. How do we know you went home?"

"Because I just told you." He blew out a plume of smoke and chuckled. He had this demeanor to him that it was all just one big joke. Skylar had a good mind to reach over and crack his head against the table but there was a guard standing by the door and she didn't fancy having to explain it to Davenport.

"That's not exactly a great alibi."

"Why are you asking?"

"Because Ted Sampson turned up dead in Otter Creek."

His eyebrows rose, and he breathed in deeply before exhaling. "Don't know anything about that."

"You ever been out to the creek?"

His brow furrowed together. "Of course. Lars took me out there multiple times."

"So you and your cousin are close?" Harvey asked.

He pulled a face as if he was unsure, but it contradicted with what he said next. "We're tight."

"Tight enough to cover up a murder he committed?"

He exhaled smoke through his nostrils and chuckled. "Oh, detective, you are going to have to come up with more than a cup of coffee and cigarettes if you think I would throw my boy under the bus."

Harvey smiled and picked at his tooth. "You've got to be looking at, at least seven years, maybe fifteen for attempted armed robbery. Not to mention assault on an officer and... well..." He gazed around the room. "You could be in here a long time. So are you sure you don't know anything?"

"Positive." He lifted up his cuffs to indicate to the guard that he wanted to leave. As he got up he smirked. "Best of luck, detective. I hope you don't lose your head trying to find the killer." He laughed and Harvey clenched his jaw. The door slammed behind him and they sat there in silence.

Chapter 13

It felt like they were spinning their wheels. Though they had concrete evidence that supported the initial theory that he was murdered, there was little to connect either Jackson or Watson to the murder. Like her, Harvey had a strong feeling that they were involved and it was eating away at him. She could tell his mind was distracted as they drove away from the correctional institution. When they got back to the department, Harvey said he was going to follow up with Hanson and speak with Rachel again, see if there anything that he'd overlooked in the computer records.

That afternoon, on her way over to speak to Laura Jennings, her cell rang. She glanced down at the display and saw that it was Scot. She pulled off to the side of the road and answered.

"Hey, how you holding up?"

"Well, it's not New York, that's for sure."

"But it's good, right? Laid back, relaxed."

"Oh, it's laid back but not relaxed. We're dealing with a murder investigation at the moment. The medical examiner turned up without a head."

"Gruesome. Got any leads yet?"

"We're making steady progress. Though things work a lot different here."

"And what about Ben? How did that go? He said you were closed off to him."

"He's been speaking with you?"

"Of course. Look, I was chatting with the powers that be back here. They know you're speaking with a psychologist. Depends on how it goes, you could get your job back here if you wanted to."

She chuckled and looked out across the bay. Several gulls screeched wheeling overhead. The sun glistened off the surface making her squint.

"Had you said that the day after I parted ways, I might have jumped on it but now, I don't know, Scot. Maybe this place is best for me. I mean going back to that would only…"

"Bring back the memories. I get it. Well, then, how's my baby doing?"

"Your boat, you mean?"

"Do I have any other baby?"

"She's still afloat, I haven't taken it out and I doubt I will."

In the background she could hear the noise of city life — the honking of horns, hotdog vendors yelling and New Yorkers grumbling. At one time she thrived on the electricity of it all but now that had changed. Being in Carrabelle had given her time to reflect, unwind and now what seemed like an escape was beginning to feel like home.

"Look, I can't speak long, some of us have to work for a living."

He laughed. "You missed a great raid this morning. We bust into this place, and this gal is completely butt naked."

"Okay, Scot, gotta go."

"But I was just getting to the best bit."

"Bye." She clicked off and sat there for a second with a grin on her face. If she was honest, she did miss the adrenaline of bursting into a house and her banter with Scot but it was time for something new. Change was in the air. She could feel it even if she was struggling to adapt to life without Alex.

Laura Jennings lived in a mobile home park on the west side of town. Harvey told her that most of the residents there were on low incomes. Cops were called out to the place at all hours of the day. A good portion of those living in the park were in the system and had been busted for drugs or prostitution, others were there because they'd lost their homes in the financial crisis. He'd warned her in advance to not make fun of any of the residents, or do anything that would offend them. "There's good people living in that park, not all of them are druggies." She had to wonder how Harvey viewed her. She wasn't a troublemaker though she did enjoy stirring the pot once in a while. As she swerved into the sandy patch of land framed by pines and cypress trees, she noticed a number of residents were sitting outside drinking beer. A faded American flag flapped in the breeze near the administration office. She weaved her way down past prefabricated single-story homes. They were much different to the conventional brick and mortar or clapboard ones she'd seen around town. Most of them had tiny gardens that were covered in kids' toys and bags of garbage, though some residents had taken the time to make their place look nice. She could see now what he was saying about the difference. It was easy to spot the parents that didn't look out for their kids as they were the ones zipping across the road with no one watching. Skylar slammed her brakes on, narrowly missing a kid about six years old who had run out to grab a ball.

"You okay, hon?" Skylar yelled out the window. She smiled, but it soon changed when an oversize woman grabbed a hold of her by the wrist and dragged her away, smacking her on the ass and cursing in front of her.

Eventually she found Laura's home on the far side of

the park, it was nestled into a corner hedged in by palm trees. There was a bicycle laying on the front lawn and an old Chevy truck with less rust than hers in the driveway.

Three boys on bikes shot past. She waited a second before pushing out. From the driveway she could hear loud music playing inside her home. AC/DC's "Thunder Struck" seeped from beyond the door. There was a wind chime blowing in the breeze outside. Dust-covered blinds covered the windows.

Skylar cast a glance around the lot and noticed an old-timer sitting in a folding chair watching her. All he was wearing was a pair of underpants, black socks, sandals and a sun hat. He was sipping on iced tea and he grinned and ran a hand over his oversize belly. She grimaced and pulled back the storm door before knocking.

There was no answer at first, so she pounded again.

Ricky appeared behind the small window and peered out. He unlocked the door and stepped out. Her senses were attacked by a waft of weed. It was real dank. Ricky was wearing a Metallica T-shirt and jeans. He closed the door behind him and Skylar noticed he had a welt on the side of his eye.

"You been fighting again, Ricky?"

His cheeks went flushed, and he touched the side of his face. "Oh. Um."

"Who is it, Ricky?" Laura's voice bellowed out.

"This is really not a good time," Ricky said. "Come back later."

"I'm here to see your mother."

"She's preoccupied."

The door swung open and standing there was a middle-aged guy, plaid shirt, dirty white undershirt and he was in the process of doing up his belt. "Ricky, your mother's calling you. You better get in."

He came out and brushed past Skylar giving her a dirty look. He slipped into the Chevy truck, lit a cigarette and fired it up all the while keeping his eyes on her. Country music blared from his speakers as he backed out, one arm stretched over the passenger seat headrest. He hit the brakes only to shout out the window, "You not hear me,

Ricky?" The door was still open and Ricky looked hesitant to go back in.

"Look, I gotta go."

"Tell your mother I want to speak to her," Skylar said.

Ricky went inside, closing the door behind him but leaving it just slightly ajar. Skylar watched the guy back out, straighten out the truck and drive about six homes down before pulling in and getting out. She shook her head. He redefined laziness.

"How many times have I told you to stay out when I have a client?"

She could hear her slapping him. He was crying and telling his mother he was sorry. He couldn't even get the words out. Skylar pushed open the door and stepped inside. The first thing she saw was a bag of weed on the counter.

"Enough," she said.

Laura still had hold of Ricky's wrist. He was slumped against the sofa and she was looming over him preventing him from protecting himself. She was dressed in nothing more than a pair of black panties and a bra. She had bruises on her legs, and one on her back. Her hair was done up, and she had a thick layer of makeup on.

"What the hell are you doing in my home?" she bellowed while trudging towards Skylar shaking her finger. She cursed and yelled, "Get out!"

"I need to speak to you." She glanced over at Ricky then back at her. "Outside."

"I've told you everything I know. Now do I need to sue the department to get them to leave me alone?"

Skylar grabbed a hold of her arm as she raised it. "I would advise you…"

She didn't even need to finish what she was about to say, Laura lowered her hand as if suddenly snapping out of whatever drug-induced fog she was in.

"Get dressed. Outside!" Skylar said stepping back out. Ricky was obviously scared as he slipped past his mother and ducked out before she could grab him. While Laura was getting some clothes on, Ricky sat on the front step tossing small pebbles at his bike. It made a pinging sound like icy rain hitting a car.

"Ricky, how often does she hit you?"

He shrugged. "Not often, just when she's been drinking or has a client over."

Even if a kid was being hit every day, five times a day, they would probably say the same thing. She knew, as her mother was an alcoholic, driven to it by her father. That was the crazy thing about having a parent who didn't measure up. At the end of the day, if given the choice, a kid would pick their abusive parent over having none at all. At least, that was the way it was with her.

"A client?"

He tossed her a glance, and he didn't need to explain. Skylar exhaled hard. It frustrated her to no end. Sure, working a regular job wasn't easy. People got laid off all the time but resorting to selling one's body for money, she couldn't figure out how anyone could stoop that low unless they were feeding an addiction. And by the looks of the dark marks on Laura's arms, she wasn't just hooked on weed.

The door opened and Laura was dressed in a thin dress and flats, and she'd wiped away the makeup she had on. She was even wearing glasses. No doubt, trying hard to win the mother of the year award. A little too late, Skylar thought.

"Ricky, go inside," his mother said.

"I'm going to my friend's."

He got up and picked his bike up and pedaled away.

"Ricky!" she said in a loud voice then lowered her tone realizing she was under Skylar's watchful eye. Laura shook her head and clenched her jaw. She folded her arms and pursed her lips. "So? What can I do for you?"

"Well you can start by stop hitting your kid. This is the second time I've had to tell you."

"I don't know where you're from, lady, but it's not illegal in Florida to spank a child."

"No, you're right — to a point," Skylar said. Laura's eyes flared. "Corporal discipline of a child for disciplinary purposes does not constitute abuse as long as it doesn't result in harm to the child. And 'harm' doesn't just mean the welt on Ricky's eye but physical, mental or emotional harm even if there is no actual bruising."

She started back at her blankly.

"I didn't mean to harm him."

"Really?" Skylar stifled a chuckle. It wasn't that it was funny, but she'd heard that line enough times. "Whether you intend to cause injury or not, if the discipline is 'likely to result' in an injury that goes beyond the scope of what is allowed, it means criminal charges can be pressed against you."

Her chin dropped. "He's my only kid."

"Well then maybe you should treat him better."

She got this expression of attitude on her face, a hand rested on one hip and she pursed her lips. "Look, are you here to bust my chops over how I raise my son or was there something else?"

"Where were you two nights ago between ten and midnight?"

Her brow pinched together and for a few seconds she said nothing then an eyebrow shot up. "Oh what? You think I was involved in that man's death?" She chuckled. "Lady, you have some nerve coming out here."

"Where were you?"

"I was here with a friend."

"A client or a friend?"

Laura narrowed her eyes and her whole demeanor shifted. "That's none of your damn business."

"In fact it is when we have someone dead whose death resembles your husband's. You left out the part the other morning about him working for Lars Jackson, or that Lars had spoken to him about the way he was treating you."

"The police already had that. Besides, that was a while ago."

Skylar stepped forward. "You see, here's the strange part in all of this. I looked at the file case on your husband and the boat he was using belonged to Lars. Now I spoke with him earlier today and he said that Tucker wasn't into fishing. In fact, he said that he was the one who got him into it after you encouraged him. And that most of the time he wasn't interested. 'He would have rather been down at the bar,' I believe his words were. So it got me thinking. Why was he out there by himself? That was what you said, right? Tucker was out there by himself fishing and a gator got him. Of course, we don't know if it was a gator as his head was never found. Guessing there must be some gator out there that only enjoys heads. And strangely enough the autopsy report was very similar to Ted's death. Do you see where I'm going with this?"

She shook her head and folded her arms even tighter in front of her chest. "No, actually I don't. What has this to do with me?"

"You know, Laura, things could get real difficult for Ricky if it came out that you were somehow involved in the death of your husband, and Ted Sampson. The state would probably take him away from you and put him into the system. So is there anything you want to tell me?"

"How dare you. How dare you!" She stabbed a finger in front of Skylar's face. "You come down here, shame me on how I raise my son, make accusations against me in regards to my late husband."

She raised her voice even louder.

"I told the police everything I knew at the time. Just because my boy found his body that doesn't mean I was involved, or that Lars has anything to do with it."

"Laura, everything okay?" A male voice from behind them yelled.

Skylar turned and saw the same guy who'd been in her home walking up with two other hefty-looking guys. All of them had tattoos and two of them were drinking beer. She could see this was going to turn sour real fast.

Laura narrowed her eyes. "Oh, I'm okay but this cop is accusing me of murdering Tucker and that medical examiner."

"Is that right?"

Skylar pulled back her jacket to give a clear view of her weapon. She wasn't in any way unnerved by the men heading her way. Unlike regular cops, every day on the job as a U.S. Marshal she had been inserted into situations that were volatile. She'd got used to the surge of adrenaline rushing through her, and the threat of violent men.

Common sense, however, needed to prevail in a situation like this. Skylar threw up a hand. "Laura, no one is accusing you of murder. But in regards to your son, it's pretty obvious what is going on. I caught you in the act. So if you want to play hardball, we can do that too. Turn around, you're under arrest for abuse leading to physical harm of a child."

"What?"

Laura began to protest as she turned her, pulled her cuffs and locked them on her before the three men had got within fifty feet. Out the corner of her eye she saw one of them throw down a beer can. Another one broke into a run heading towards her. With one hand on the cuffs and pushing Laura up against the mobile home, she reached for her firearm and pulled it. Keeping it low and not pointed at them, she locked on them. "I would advise you all to back off. Go back to your homes."

"And if we don't?"

"Try me," Skylar said.

There were a tense few minutes before they began backing up. Meanwhile Laura was still yelling at the top of her voice and cursing. Skylar strong-armed her over to her truck.

"What about my boy?"

Skylar looked off farther down the road. Ricky was talking with a couple of friends, he looked their way and got on his bike and started pedaling fast towards them. "Mom? What's going on?"

Instead of acting like a caring mother, she started blaming and cursing at him. "This is your fault. You should have kept your mouth closed."

Skylar assisted her into the passenger side of her truck and slammed the door closed muting the barrage of curse words directed towards her and her son. She turned and approached him.

"Please. Just let her go. I don't—"

"Ricky, you want her to hit you again?"

His gaze bounced between her and his mother. She could see he was conflicted. He shook his head. "I just don't want her getting in trouble."

It wasn't that. It was because he knew she'd take it out on him later.

"Look, do you have anyone you can stay with for now?"

"My grandmother, she lives just around the corner."

"Okay, go grab a few things and head on over to her."

His face screwed up. "What will happen to her?"

"That's not for me to decide. She will speak to someone from the court. Before that I need to talk with your mother first."

His chin dropped, Skylar placed a hand on his shoulder. "This isn't your fault. Okay? You understand? You don't deserve to get hit by anyone."

He nodded and went off and gathered a few belongings. Skylar jumped back into her vehicle and followed Ricky to make sure he arrived safely before she headed back to the station. All the way Laura hurled abuse at her. The woman was as high as a kite. A poor excuse for a mother. Skylar shook her head and allowed her to continue her rant. First there was anger, then there was pleading, then abuse again. She kept circling back and forth, that's why Skylar was confident that if they stuck her in an interview room, they could probably get her to tell them something. If not, she would be charged with child abuse and possession of marijuana.

Even though that would prevent her from hitting Ricky again, she couldn't help think that it really wasn't a win-win situation. No one won in a situation like this — especially a child.

Chapter 14

The afternoon passed by uneventfully. Laura refused to say anything even in light of the fact that child services and the court were going to make it difficult for her to have access to Ricky again. No surprise there. She didn't give a rat's ass about that kid. It was a sad state of affairs. Instead, she was kept in a holding cell until they could get her before a judge the next day. In the meantime they'd managed to get a warrant from a judge to search her mobile home. It was early evening by the time they received it. Harvey and Skylar headed over there eager to see what they could dig up.

Her mind was a flurry of thoughts as she tried to make connections with what they'd unearthed so far. They were still waiting to hear back from the lab regarding hair samples they'd found in the truck.

"So you never had any luck with Hanson?"

"Oh, I didn't say that, I just meant he was being

difficult."

"What's the deal with you and those two? Hanson said that you and him used to get on. Did something happen?"

"Ask him about it sometime."

"That's exactly what he said," she replied.

He scoffed as if finding something amusing.

"Anyway regarding the third bank account. It's in Ted's name. Nothing peculiar about it other than the fact that he was withdrawing and depositing large sums of money on a weekly basis."

"For what purpose?"

"That's what we're trying to establish. I can see someone taking out a couple of hundred bucks here or there to pay for items but if you purchase a computer or get some work on a vehicle, usually you pay via debit, credit card or such but he was taking out amounts of four to nine grand in cash. I spent the better part of the morning and afternoon going over his financial records with a fine-tooth comb and I can't see where he's made any large purchases. Of course he was planning on purchasing the home in Colorado but there are no receipts for anything that would have required nine thousand dollars."

"Perhaps he gave it to someone."

"It's possible, or he stashed it under his mattress. Anyway I went and spoke with Rachel again and she was dumbfounded to learn that he had these accounts. She only knew about the one, not the offshore one, or the third account or even his PayPal accounts. Rachel said that he hadn't made any large purchases. All the furniture in the home had been bought several years ago."

"So he had to have been given the money or was stashing it somewhere. But why? Why stash your own money elsewhere when you have an offshore account and online accounts to keep it in? It makes no sense unless he was hiding it from someone."

"Or giving it."

Her brow knit together. "Did you speak with the bank to find out how he took out the money? I imagine it would have set off some red flags, requesting that amount of money on a frequent basis. Most of the cash in banks is just digital."

He nodded as they pulled into the mobile home park. The sun was beginning to wane behind the cypress trees, a rich golden orange streaked the sky. Gone was the humidity of the day, now all that was left was a fresh breeze blowing in off the coast.

"Well that was my thought. So yeah, I got in contact with the bank. Seems that banks have to report any withdrawal transaction over $10,000 in cash due to the 1980 anti-money-laundering law."

"Were they able to establish if he took out money from one branch and then more from another?"

"They can see that, in fact, if he withdrew $5,000 in the morning and another $5,000 in the afternoon from a different branch, that would trigger a report to the IRS. And if the transactions don't occur on the same day, the banks are still under obligation if they think they are related to file a report."

"Huh!" Skylar muttered as the truck made its way down to the trailer. "So that explains the different kinds of transactions he was making."

"It doesn't end there. Because they are wise to people trying to avoid triggering the Bank Secrecy Act, they also have to report transactions that are less than $10,000 when they think those transactions are specifically to avoid triggering a report. So if he went and took out $9,900 that would raise a red flag. There are only a few exceptions and that is if the person is a regular business customer and let's say the customer owned a department store and took out twenty grand for the store's safe or registers. In those cases they don't have to make a report each time as it's already been established why they are using it. But it requires a separate form that the bank files with the IRS and it must be renewed on a yearly basis."

He killed the engine as they parked outside. Darkness was beginning to blanket the park and her trailer had an ominous look to it.

"Which would make money laundering tough to do,

and yet everything about the way he has things set up would lead me to believe that's exactly what he was doing," Skylar said.

They sat in the vehicle for a moment contemplating it.

"But we don't have definite proof right now to start making accusations."

"Think about it, Harvey. How many other online gambling companies have been charged with using their service as a means to launder money?"

He turned towards her. "You don't even need to ask. I looked it up today. It seems that online gambling is harder to regulate and there have been a number of incidents."

"And if you wanted to do it successfully without drawing attention to yourself, how would you do that?" she asked. They looked at each other and gave the same answer.

"Bring on board a group of investors."

"That's right. Banks are going to red flag one person but bring in ten, twenty, or more, so there are more people involved performing different transactions from different banks. Then to add to that, let's consider that you select investors that already have an addiction to gambling and now you have a network that can launder your money without red flags."

Harvey said, "And what do investors love? Guaranteed returns. Nothing is better than playing for money which you are guaranteed to win in a game that you already love. If the odds are in your favor, who's to say you didn't win that money legitimately? No one is going to question it. You got online, played a few games, won a tidy sum, it got transferred into your payment processor, you then transfer to a bank and take out several thousand every couple of days or weeks. No red flags." He paused. "That has to be why so many investors on that list he gave me were willing to shell out money to invest in a new start-up."

Skylar clicked her fingers and pushed out of the truck. She breathed in deeply chewing it all over. It was a simple case of following the leads. There was always a trail and in this case, there were several. "That leaves only one question. Where is the money coming from? If they were laundering it through the gambling site, it had to be flowing in from somewhere." She paused for a second. "What do Tito Martinez and Lars Jackson have in common?" She leaned across the lip of her truck. Harvey was on the other side doing the same.

"Drug trafficking."

Chapter 15

"I hope you have a warrant to search that place," a male voice hollered as they were making their way over to the Jennings trailer. Skylar turned to the see the same guy she'd had a run-in with earlier that day. Of course he looked two sheets to the wind. He was holding a beer in a brown paper bag and looked a little wobbly on his feet. Harvey pulled out the warrant.

"And who might you be?"

He wandered over, cigarette in hand. He was about five six, still wearing the same dirty outfit he had on earlier. The laces in his boots were untied and he kept stumbling a little. "Bud Jennings."

"Related to Laura?"

"She's my sister-in-law."

"Oh, so you're Tucker's brother."

"Yeah. What y'all doing here anyway?"

His breath smelled like cigarettes and alcohol. He

burped and stumbled back a bit.

"Following up. You look like you've had one too many, why don't you go sleep it off?" Harvey said turning away from him and about to head over to the trailer.

"Why don't you go screw yourself?"

Skylar heard a sound behind her and saw a light shining inside the mobile home. "Anyone else staying with Laura?" Harvey asked.

"No, Ricky went to his grandmother's."

They approached the trailer, and she pulled open the door. Meanwhile, Bud was still hurling insults and telling them he wasn't done with them, and how badly they'd screwed up the investigation of his brother's death. Skylar stepped in just in time to catch a glimpse of someone slipping out the back window.

"Harv, around back. Go!"

"What?"

He hadn't even made it inside so he had no clue what she was yelling about.

"Just follow me."

She burst out of the door and broke into a sprint. Under the cover of darkness it was hard to see who it was. All she could make out was the silhouette of someone hauling ass out of there. They broke away from the rear of the home into a thick wall of pines.

"Police, stop!" Skylar yelled but the figure paid no attention. They darted in and out of the trees, barreling through thick underbrush. She pulled her Glock and kept it low as she ran at a crouch. The individual burst out of the trees and double-timed it through the mobile home park. Now she could see they were wearing a red hoodie and a leather jacket with black sneakers. She gave several commands for them to stop but they refused to listen. She motioned for Harvey to go one way while she went the other. She figured if she cut through the mobile home park heading in the same direction she'd eventually cut them off before they reached the exit. Her heart pounded in her chest and sweat formed on her brow as she vaulted over garbage and toys residents had left outside their homes. She cursed under her breath. There wasn't much light inside the park, only the glow from people's homes and the light of the moon. In between the homes she could see the figure looking over their shoulder towards Harvey who was closing in. Skylar tucked her piece back into her holster and darted through a narrow walkway behind two homes.

A surge of adrenaline and she burst out of the opening and plowed into the individual knocking them to the ground, they rolled across the road and came to a halt just outside someone's front door. The person groaned.

"Get off."

"Ricky?"

She took her knee off his back and yanked his hood back just as Harvey caught up, his flashlight swept over his face.

"Holy cow. I could have shot you. Why the hell were you running?"

Harvey bent down and pulled at his pocket. "I think I have an idea."

He straightened up and flashed the light on a bag of

weed. It was the same one from earlier that day. Her eyes bounced from the bag to him. "That was yours?"

"So I smoke some pot every once in a while. Big deal. Lots of kids my age do."

Harvey chuckled. "Didn't they tell you to not admit to it? First rule of pot club. There is no pot." He shook his head and laughed as Skylar helped Ricky to his feet. He got up and his jeans were covered in grass stains. He brushed off dirt from his top.

"Did you touch anything else inside?"

"No, I was just…" He cursed, his chin dropped.

"Does this belong to your mother or to you?"

"I bought it."

"But she used it."

He snorted. "You've got to be kidding. She was all about shooting up."

Skylar squeezed the bridge of her nose and sighed as they made their way back to the trailer. She was disappointed but not surprised. Anyone under his conditions would have looked for ways to fade out.

Marijuana was minor even though possession of 20 grams or less was considered a misdemeanor and was punishable up to a maximum sentence of one year's imprisonment and a fine of $1,000. However, because he was a juvenile, there was a good chance he'd qualify for a diversion program. Still, it wasn't something he needed on his record, and with all the crap that was going on with his mother, she wasn't sure if it was even worth bringing to the department's attention. She figured she could use her discretion to caution him due to it being a minor offense.

When they made it back to the truck, she told Ricky to get in and she would drop him off at his grandmother's. As soon as she said it, Harvey scowled, and she had a feeling what was going through his head. She slammed the door closed, and he grabbed a hold of her arm.

"What are you doing? We need to take him in."

"He's just a kid, Harv."

"Doesn't matter. The punishment down in the Sunshine State is stiff for these things."

She snorted. "You're telling me you never once smoked weed when you were a kid?"

He shifted from one foot to the next. Skylar's eyes darted to Ricky who was watching it all play out in front of him. Thankfully Bud had wandered back to his abode. She didn't fancy having to argue with him and Harvey.

"Not once."

"Please. And I guess you're going to tell me you never looked up porn either."

She turned to walk into the mobile home.

"Hold up. Skylar!"

She twisted around.

"Down here we do things by the book. You might be used to something different where you come from but we have laws here for a reason."

"Yeah, and it says that we can caution. It's his first offense. At least I think it is."

"First. Second. You let him off the hook now and he will think he can do it again. Maybe next time he will be high behind a wheel. What then? What will you tell a loved one when their family member died because he was behind a wheel high, huh?"

"Oh God, Harv, stop being so dramatic. He's fifteen for God's sake!"

"Then he'll be sixteen, seventeen, eighteen and then what?"

Skylar paused on the steps looking down. She turned back to him and jabbed her finger into his chest. "You ever get knocked around when you were a kid, Harvey? Huh? Did your mother or father beat you so hard that you couldn't go to school because of the bruising?"

He bristled. "No."

"Well I did. Yeah, I know what it's like to be on the other end of a mother who drank too much and spent what little we had on booze. A woman who locked me in my room just so she could get drunk and not have to be reminded of what was her responsibility."

She studied his face, looking for some kind of response. His lips moved as if he was going to say something but nothing came out.

"You want him to end up like Bud Jennings, or his old man? Go ahead. Book him. Put him through the system. Hell, he might end up there anyway because of what his mother did today. So why not throw another log on the fire and stir it up real hot?"

He stared back blankly. She turned around and walked into the mobile home to begin the search. She was done trying to convince him. They had the official right as a police officer to use discretion for minor offenses and if ever there was a time that they needed to use it, it was now. But she couldn't force him to agree. If he wouldn't go along with it, well, it looked like they would be booking him. Harvey stayed outside with the kid while she went about searching the inside. She flipped a switch to turn the electricity on but it didn't come on. Surprise, surprise, she thought. Probably spent the money on drugs. Skylar snapped on some blue latex gloves, brought out her flashlight and flicked it on. The light washed over the dark corners. Over the course of the next half an hour she tore that place apart. Lifted the mattress, looked under the bed, in cupboards, inside cereal boxes and metal containers, checked in the tank of the toilet, under the sink and some of the most common areas that people hid items they didn't want anyone finding.

The search didn't turn up much, just some drug paraphernalia, a laptop, a small baggie of coke and some unpaid parking tickets — all of which was out in the open. It was like she either didn't expect anyone from the department to knock on her door or she didn't care. There certainly wasn't more than 28 grams, which would have landed her a first-degree felony. Chances were she would do some time in the county jail if it was her first offense and qualify for some diversion program. The question was where had she got the coke?

When she exited the trailer Harvey was leaning against her truck on the phone to someone. She gathered what she'd collected and put it into evidence bags and returned to the truck. He ended the call and looked over.

"So?"

She cast a glance at him. "Not much. I don't expect

she'll give up the name of her dealer or even if it's related to money laundering. Though we might pull something off the laptop. Who were you on the phone to?"

"The department. No record on Ricky, or Laura. Seems they have kept their noses clean up to this point."

She went over to the passenger side and opened the door.

"This yours?" She asked lifting the Mac so he could see it.

Ricky shook his head. "My mom's."

She looked off towards where Bud's home was. "Ricky. Listen. As this is your first offense, I'm going to let you off with a warning."

"Do I get to keep the weed?"

"Don't push it!"

He offered back a thin smile. "So I'm free to go?"

She nodded. "But under one condition. Who did you get it from?"

He squinted and looked away.

"Come on, Ricky. Who did you buy it from?"

He picked at a loose strand of his jeans.

"Ricky."

"I didn't buy it. It was given to me."

"That's mighty generous. By who?"

She could see the muscles in his jaw clench.

"Look, I'm going out on a limb here for you. I can't help you if you don't help me. Anyone who is willing to put you in the line of fire isn't worth a lick of salt. So who is it?"

He ran a hand around the back of his neck and scratched. "Will he get in trouble?"

"That depends. Come on, tell me."

"Lars."

"Lars Jackson?"

He nodded and locked eyes with her.

"And did he provide your mother with her stash too?"

That made him real uncomfortable. He shifted in his seat and cleared his throat. "Look, I don't know about that. All I know is that he had some extra, and he gave me what was left. Said it was okay, and it was his way of doing good by me."

"Because he was seeing your mother?"

He shrugged. He genuinely didn't seem to know.

She breathed in deeply. "All right. Just give me a minute and I'll take you back to your grandma's. And remember, Ricky. No more. Next time, it might not be me busting you and the officer might not be as lenient."

She closed the door and went over to Harvey who had been listening in.

"Seems we need to pay Lars Jackson another visit. If he's handing it out, makes you wonder if he has more than enough to go around. Is it me or does a picture seem to be taking shape?" she asked.

"If he's distributing, he's not going to have any of it down at his place of business. The Jacksons have got smarter than that. If the '80s taught them anything, it was not to be caught with it or selling it."

"How did they go about it back then?"

Harvey leaned his back against the front of her truck. "Oh it was quite an operation they were running. You have got to remember, weed was the big thing back in the '80s. It was a lot more prevalent than it is today, especially with states legalizing it. The black market isn't as lucrative as it used to be. It's mostly cocaine and heroin today. Anyway back in those days they would have a crew of boats that would head out into the Gulf and meet a large cargo ship that would unload barrels of it, they would collect it and head back through the Thousand Islands just south of Everglades City. It would then be transported to trucks and then they would take it to Miami and have distributors there sell it for them." He breathed in deeply. "July 7, 1983, Operation Everglades. It was one of the biggest drug busts in Florida. Two hundred federal drug agents and county sheriff's deputies had been working the case for close to two years. Interesting part is that the town had been the center of rum smuggling back in the Prohibition era. I guess they figured they would just continue the tradition."

Skylar glanced at her watch. It was getting late. They wouldn't hear back from the lab on fibers and anything else they'd managed to find until tomorrow so her plan was to put what she'd collected into evidence and call it a day.

"You think they are back in the game?"

Harvey snorted. "I don't think they ever stopped playing."

Chapter 16

Early the next morning, three days into the investigation, Skylar met with Harvey, hopeful that they were drawing closer to uncovering the killer. They'd spent the better part of an hour having breakfast and discussing the case down at the Carrabelle Junction. Barb was adamant that she was going to convince Skylar that there was no other place in the town that could make coffee like hers. She was on her second cup and had just put away a tasty breakfast when Harvey got the call from the lab. Although the results confirmed what the autopsy report had said, which was Ted was strangled, it was where they'd managed to find ligature fibers which had been connected as a perfect match to the microscopic fibers found imbedded in Ted's neck skin, or what was left of it.

"You're certain?" Harvey said with the phone up to his ear. He lowered his cup of coffee, thanked them for calling and then clicked off.

"So?"

"Seems fibers from the rope that was used to strangle Ted were found on his clothing, in the truck as well as in the boat belonging to Lars Jackson, even though that boat was in the possession of Ricky that morning. The lab believed it to be a match."

She downed the rest of her coffee. "Well, that certainly is going to be hard to explain." Skylar screeched her chair back to get up and leave. "Time to head over to Lars's place and have a heart-to-heart."

"Hold up, Skylar. After Hanson was able to collect that boot print, I had them match it with Cole Watson's clothing the day he was booked. They've got a match."

She stopped at the door, her hand on the handle. "So he was at the scene?"

"Appears so."

"And there was me thinking this was going to be a closed case by midday today."

"We need to go have another chat with Cole."

She nodded, and they headed out for the Carrabelle Correctional Institution. Along the way Harvey got on the phone to speak with the dive team who hadn't been updated and were still in the thick of trying to locate Ted's head, as well as what might have been used in the strangulation. They'd spent hours wading through that swamp unearthing garbage that fishermen over the years had dumped or dropped. None of it was connected to the case. By all accounts they were making more progress outside the water with Ted's financial trail than with what might have been used to murder him. Although finding fibers confirmed he'd been strangled, without the actual rope it was like having the bullet without the gun. However, it did present a new line of questions that Lars would need to be able to answer, such as: How did rope fibers that are a match to a murder victim end up in one of his boats? Still, finding a boot print matching Cole Watson's at the scene and in the truck was the most damning evidence as he'd insisted that he was at home at the time of the murder, and this would place him at the scene.

They swung by the department on the way over to collect the photos taken from the scene, along with those that had been taken from Cole's boots.

They arrived outside the institution just after 8:30 a.m. They kind of figured Cole was going to deny it, but they had to gauge his reaction, see what he might say. If there was any time that he might be willing to speak it would be now. Cole had this swagger to him as he walked in as if he wasn't fazed by prison.

"Detectives, really, I'm not lonely in here. You don't have to visit all the time," he said smirking as he took a seat. He scanned the table. "What? No coffee or cigarettes today?" He pulled a face and leaned back. "Guessing you aren't expecting much out of me then."

Skylar was the first to start questioning. "Three nights ago you said you were at home but we have evidence that places you in Otter Creek Swamp. Now you want to tell us how that is?"

He got this smile on his face. "Evidence? What kind of

evidence?"

"Your boot print." She opened up a folder and tossed two images before him, one taken from the outside of the vehicle and the other from inside.

"I fish all the time out of Otter Creek, that doesn't mean squat."

"Your boot print was also found in the locked truck of Ted Sampson's vehicle found at the scene. So you want to explain that?"

"I don't even know who Ted Sampson is."

Skylar chuckled and leaned back in her seat, she cast a glance at Harvey and he leaned forward. "Cole, it won't take long before we can determine that your DNA was found all over that truck, on the murder weapon and maybe even the body. So you want to stop jerking us around. How did your boot print wind up there?"

He leaned back tapping the table.

Harvey pressed him further. "It's one thing to go away for armed robbery but murder, you would be in here for life. Do you want that?"

He sneered back. "Screw you, Baker. You've had it out for me since the first day you laid eyes on me." He laughed. "You ain't got nothing on me. Anyone could have worn boots the same as me."

Harvey banged his fist on the table. "There is a kid that's without a father. Now it's time you start telling us what you know."

His leg started shaking, and he looked up at the clock. "I don't think it's in my best interest to be speaking to you without a lawyer. I want a lawyer. That's it. I'm not saying another word because I know how you work. You are just going to twist what I say. You are desperate and you need someone to blame. You're going to make me a scapegoat. Well, I'm not being laid on a sacrificial altar. Not for this. I might have done a lot of stupid things in my time but murder? You really think I would do that?"

"You held a loaded gun up to my head. I believe you're capable of anything."

He leaned forward clasping his hands together. "I didn't do it! He was dead when I got there," he spat out.

Not even a second after he had blurted it out in anger, he realized he'd screwed up. "I mean…"

Skylar knew what he meant; the question was if he was lying.

"You were there that morning, weren't you? With Ricky?"

His eyes darted from Harvey to her and then dropped.

"I didn't kill him. I swear. I took Ricky out. He wanted to go out, Lars was busy that morning, so he had me take the boat out there and go fishing with the kid. I swear on my mother's life. That is what happened."

"So how did your boot end up inside his vehicle?"

He sucked his bottom lip in, his mangled top teeth biting down hard. She could see the expression of regret.

"When we came across the body, it was near the edge of the shore. I brought the boat in and went over to the truck. It was unlocked at the time. The door was wide open. I… uh… saw the note there and the bottle of drink and checked inside for money. I know, stupid, right? I swear I didn't touch anything. I just rooted through the vehicle to see if there was any money."

"And was there?"

"Twenty dollars. I took it."

Harvey snorted, shaking his head.

"So why did you lock the doors?"

"I didn't, I just slammed the door closed. It must have been set to lock."

"And what did you do after that?"

He scratched his forehead and breathed in deeply. "I figured the kid wouldn't get in trouble because he doesn't have a record. If I had called it in, no one would have believed me with my rap sheet. They would have hauled me in for his murder. But I swear he was dead when we arrived that morning. I was at home that night."

Harvey got up from his seat and paced around the room. "You know the way this looks, right? You don't have an alibi for where you were other than telling us you were at home. You lied to us about being at the scene and now you expect us to believe that you weren't involved."

"I wasn't. You gotta believe me, man. Ask the kid.

He'll vouch for me."

"He lied for you. The question is why?" Harvey muttered.

Skylar remained stoic staring at him as Harvey continued to bombard him with questions and circle around the same answers. Then something dawned on her. "You gave Ricky marijuana, didn't you?"

Cole Watson's eyes flashed back to her.

"You asked him not to say anything and in return you gave him a bag of weed. He didn't get it from Lars, did he?"

At first he said nothing. His head dropped, then he looked up at the clock on the wall.

"Shouldn't I have my lawyer here?"

Skylar was quick to try and put him at ease. "Look, if you didn't do it, what do you have to worry about? Okay, you lied previously but if you're telling the truth now…"

He swung his handcuffed hands around as though he was swatting a fly in front of his face. "I am telling the truth. I didn't kill that man. Hell, I didn't even know him. Why would I kill someone I don't even know?" He glared at Harvey again.

"Maybe because you're a drug-addicted loser!" Harvey bellowed.

Cole cursed at him and told him where to go.

Skylar got up and motioned with her head towards the door. He was reluctant but eventually he stepped outside.

"What the hell are you doing? We have him. You need to lay aside whatever personal issues you have so we can get him to speak. You know as well as I do the second a lawyer steps in here, he is going to tighten up like a cat's ass. Now are you okay to go back in there?"

Harvey gritted his teeth and she could see he was fuming. He shook his head. "I need to get some air."

"Yeah, go do that. I'll speak to him."

She watched as Harvey walked away. He kicked a trash can on his way out and she had to wonder what kind of history he had in the town prior to her arrival. If he'd spent his entire life here, he would have rubbed shoulders with all kinds. She realized Ted was a good friend of his, it would have been like losing Scot.

Skylar composed herself and shook off the feeling of animosity towards Cole before she returned. This time, however, she brought with her a cup of coffee. While they were out, she figured he would have been berating himself for blurting out what he had, and probably thinking of how he could squirm his way out of the tight spot.

"Here, do you need a cigarette?"

She'd purchased a pack on the way just in case he started playing hardball. As clichéd as it may have seemed, it was amazing how quickly someone would open up if put in a situation where they felt relaxed, and for an addict, nothing did it quite like the rush of nicotine, and a healthy dose of caffeine.

He cracked a smile. "So you get to play the good cop today, do you?"

"Something like that."

She lit the cigarette, and he breathed in deeply. Almost immediately his shoulders relaxed, and he leaned back and shook his head. "You know, detective, there was a time I didn't have a record. My mother always said that I was a good kid." He shook his head again as if he was reliving the past in his mind. His eyes closed tight as he took another drag and smoke poured from his nostrils after the hit.

"Yeah, I gave him the weed."

"Okay, now we're making progress. So Ricky told us that Lars had given it to him so that was just to cover up for you. Tell me, were you seeing Laura on the side?"

He blew out more smoke and his eyes widened. "Are you kidding me? That woman has been double-dipped more times than a bowl of artichoke dip at a Super Bowl party. Hell, I wouldn't get near her with a barge pole. That is just damn nasty." He chuckled.

"So why would you agree to take Ricky out fishing?"

His eyebrows arched. "Other than the fact that I like fishing?" He sniffed hard. "Lars paid me to. It was either that or spend the day out taking a bunch of whiny tourists around the bay, and after the night I had before, no, that wasn't happening."

"You get drunk that night?"

"Just a little."

"That something regular for you?"

"We all have our vices, detective. So do you."

His words cut into her. He was right. She wasn't much better. Since losing Alex and the baby she'd spiraled into all forms of self-deprecating behavior. Drinking was one of them. However, if she was really honest, it hadn't started with the tragedy, it had become a coping mechanism that she'd picked up from her parents.

"So you worked for Lars?"

"On and off, yeah. He wouldn't hire me full-time. Said I was unreliable." He shrugged. "Can't blame him, I guess, but yeah, I helped him out when he needed me. It was enough to pay rent each month so I couldn't complain."

She studied him, trying to search for cracks in his façade. Although they were aware, he'd withheld information that was vital to the case, she didn't get the sense that he was lying now. He didn't have to admit to the marijuana, but he did. Perhaps he was trying to clear his conscience. Criminals were known to do that once they couldn't see a way out. Then it all became about lessening the blow of the justice system, and without a doubt the more he assisted the stronger his chance was of receiving a reduced sentence. They all knew how it worked.

"Tell me, is Lars a gambler?"

She wanted to ask a more direct question. One that might connect him with Royal City but she didn't want to push her luck. Already what they'd managed to get out of Cole was helpful. He leaned forward and smirked. "Who isn't, detective?"

"So did you and him toss down a few bills with Royal City?"

"Oh you bet. Except when Lars plays, it's not a few bills. That guy has the luck of the Irish."

"What kind of money are we talking about?"

"Thousands every week. Yeah, I told him, I don't know why he continues to run his business. He could pay others to do it and he could sit back in the lap of luxury, drink beers and—"

"Thank you, Cole."

Skylar's chair screeched back as she got up to leave.

"Hold on a second. What about my deal?"

"What deal?"

Chapter 17

Harvey was drinking coffee and chatting with one of the guards when Skylar blew past him. "Let's go, Harv."

"What?"

He tossed his coffee in the garbage and hurried to catch up. She was already outside the building by the time he fell in step. "Skylar, what's going on?"

She hopped into the driver's side and fired up the engine. Her mind flipped through numerous scenarios. She was connecting what she'd been told along with the evidence in order to discover who she believed was behind the murder. She ignored Harvey's repeated demand to know what was going on as the truck tore away from the prison.

"Skylar, would you slow down and tell me what is going on?"

"We didn't get the CCTV footage from stores in the area, did we?"

"No, I was going to have Reznik do it but we've been a little busy."

"The list of investors William gave you. Ted's name was down on it, yes?"

"Yeah, and?"

"Was Lars on there?"

"No."

A smile cracked on her face and she nodded. "Get on the phone to the bank and see if they can pull up the last withdrawal he made and let's find out if they have any surveillance cameras on the outside of the building."

"Where are you going with this?"

"Cole admitted to being with Ricky on the morning the body was found. He admits to going inside the vehicle which was open at the time, and he admits to giving weed to Ricky. I think Ted was going to see Lars that night to give him money."

"Hold on a minute. Stop the vehicle."

She fired a glance at him.

"Skylar, stop the vehicle."

She slammed the brakes and eased off to the side of the road.

"Even if it's true. Nothing has been found connecting Lars to the truck or the scene other than his boat and a few fiber strands. You can't go busting in there demanding answers. Lars might not have a team of lawyers behind him, but Callum Jackson does and believe me, all it takes is one call and Lars would be out on bail and we would be back to spinning wheels. We need more than that before we start making accusations. At least with Cole we can place him at the scene. Besides, if Ted was murdered elsewhere, like at Lars's place of business, we are going to need a warrant to search it. Hell, I would have expected you to know that." He exhaled hard and ran a hand over his face. "Skylar, this bull in a china shop approach might have worked where you came from but here it's different. I get it. You're eager to close the case but you haven't dealt with the Jacksons before."

"They're not above the law, Harvey."

"No, but they know people in high places and it's not

easy."

"What are you not telling me?" She turned in her seat as a vehicle shot by. Harvey didn't look at her, instead he continued to look on past the pines and cypress trees. Dark brooding clouds had rolled in, and the sun was trying to peek out from beneath the belly of the clouds.

"Eight years ago, we had several women that washed up on the shores of the Panhandle. Most of them were known drug users, one of them was my sister." He looked at her. "Her name was Evelyn. Unlike the others, she wasn't a user, but she worked for Callum Jackson. A few days before her body was found, she contacted me, said she was scared, and that she needed to speak to me about what was going on in her job. That she'd been holding a lot of it in because she knew I was a cop and well, she didn't want to lose her job. She never told me what was happening, and I was meant to meet with her the day before her body was found. She never showed up. Now I know that Callum was behind it."

He shook his head and clenched his jaw, and Skylar

saw him ball his fist. Now she was beginning to understand his animosity for the Jacksons and anyone associated with them. "Anyway, Hanson and Reznik had got a lead on women being used as drug mules to transport money from Franklin County to Miami and I told them to hold off one more day before they rushed in and raided the Callums' residence. I said that if they were too hasty, he would get off. And that's what happened." He exhaled hard. "I think someone in the department tipped off Callum and I believe he killed my sister thinking that she'd leaked out information."

"So that's why the relationship between you and Hanson is strained?"

He nodded while picking at his pant leg.

"If they had just listened instead of racing in there, maybe we would have been able to take them down. Instead, nothing was found, he lawyered up, and the case was thrown out. A lack of evidence they said."

Skylar squinted into the horizon as a deep southern sun beat down on the road creating heat waves that danced above the surface.

"I just want to do this right. If it was Lars or someone who worked for him, we need to play this smart. Gather as much evidence as we can to build a strong case, so that when we go in there for that warrant, we can arrest him at the same time and have a strong reason to be able to hold him. We're on the right track, Skylar, but we still need a motive."

"Let's check the surveillance from that night and find out if Hanson got anything from phone records. If Ted was involved in money laundering, perhaps Lars will show up on video."

"How do you think he's doing it?"

"I think Tito was just a contact. The Latin Syndicate has deep ties into the drug market. It's possible they were making arrangements for a drop, money is exchanged, drugs are sold on the street then that cash is given to so-called investors. They funnel the money into offshore bank accounts, push it through the digital online payment processor, then it goes through the online gambling site and maybe they have it rigged to pay out a certain amount back, so they win back what they put in plus some more. They keep the extra and they take what they originally used and put that into a separate bank account and make withdrawals and give that cash to William Akitt's company. I was looking into it last night and it seems that in many offshore jurisdictions, gamblers are not required to pay tax on their winnings."

"That's a lot of steps to clean money."

"Virtual payment systems are under less scrutiny. And just because Royal City is fronting an operation here in Carrabelle, it doesn't mean their website is here. I wouldn't be surprised if the server is outside the States. That way even if they were raided, business would continue. Now if you throw into that the ability to hide IP addresses through VPN services, anonymity increases and it becomes easier to encrypt gambling traffic and keep laundering out of law enforcement's sight."

"And if the investors are already folks who gamble, all it would take is for the company to come up with some proposition and you don't even have to worry about investors saying anything as they are guaranteed to make money."

"Exactly. We already have the money trail, we just need to see how Lars fits into all of this. So far we have his boat with a fiber inside."

"Yeah, but unless Cole was involved with the murder, they might just say that he picked it up from inside the truck that morning and transferred it there by way of his clothing. We need to know who Ted met with that night and find out if he made a withdrawal."

Skylar dropped her head back. It was getting more complex by the minute. They were so close. It was coming together but still there was something missing. Harvey was right. Of course she wasn't just going to burst into Lars's place of business and start performing a search but she was going to ruffle his feathers. It had worked in the past with fugitives they'd pursued. Sometimes applying pressure would draw them out and get them to make stupid decisions.

"The banks wouldn't have been open, so if he did withdraw, he had to do it via the ATM machine. They have cameras, we should check that."

"Yeah, I agree, but he may have already had the money on him. Let me give the bank a phone call and see if I can find out when and how much his last transaction was."

She nodded and brought the truck back out onto the road while he placed the phone call.

When they made it back to town, Harvey wanted to be dropped off at the department so he could collect his vehicle and go speak with the bank manager. He also said he would look into CCTV surveillance footage from the area. Skylar was keen to drop by Ricky's grandmother's place and have another word with him. Before she did that, she wanted to follow up on a hunch. As Harvey pulled away for his meeting, she went inside the department to try and locate Hanson. It was busy inside, several cops were writing up reports and the usual hum of the office made her feel at ease.

"Hanson," she said noticing him across the room at his

desk. Reznik was across from him on the phone. "The financial records we have for Sampson. Can I take a look at them?"

"Yeah, of course." He dug around inside his drawer and pulled out a file and handed it to her. "Any luck with Cole Watson?"

"He admits to being there but only in the morning."

"Well I guess that's something. Davenport has been riding our ass this morning. He wants an update on the investigation as Rachel has been calling and hassling the department for answers. Poor woman doesn't understand what we're dealing with here."

Skylar was half listening as she thumbed through the deposits and transfers in Ted's offshore account. Sure enough she could see a pattern. Each week he would deposit amounts between six and eight grand, he would then transfer it into his PayPal account over a period of a few days. She then checked the PayPal activity. Sure enough the same money would be used at Royal City's website, and then on the same day, he would receive back the money with extra. The extra amount of money varied from a couple of hundred to a few thousand. He would then transfer the same six to eight grand over to his other bank account and make withdrawals on that over several days. For several months everything looked the same until the last couple of weeks when he started taking out larger amounts and sending it back to his offshore account. She took a seat and brought up a calculator and did the math on how much he was taking. Over several months it was close to four hundred and ninety grand. One look at the pattern of deposits and withdrawals made it clear what was going on. He was skimming off the top, taking more than he should. She thought back to what Rachel had said about them thinking of moving to Colorado. It was starting to make sense now as to why he might have been killed. The cogs in her brain continued to make connections as she thumbed through more of the financial records.

Chapter 18

It was a simple case of firming up Cole Watson's alibi, then she would drop by Rachel's place to ask a few more questions as she hadn't been answering her phone. When Skylar pulled into a spot outside Ricky's grandmother's mobile home, her timing couldn't have been worse.

Sitting outside drinking a beer was Bud Jennings. He was talking to a woman in her mid-sixties. She had a full head of gray hair and was rocking back and forth in a chair drinking sweet tea. As soon as Bud locked eyes on Skylar, he lit a cigarette and approached her truck.

Her window was wound down so she could hear his rant long before he reached it.

"Back again. I hope you have some details on my brother's killer and you're not just here to hassle little Ricky. The kid has been through enough with his mother. What is going on with her? She says she's being held in County until she goes before a judge?"

Skylar pushed out of the vehicle and could smell the alcohol on his breath as he got close.

"I'm not in the mood, Bud. I'm here to see Ricky."

He stepped in front of her, blocking her path.

"You got a warrant?"

"Bud. Let the woman through," the older lady said. "I don't want any trouble."

He eyed her with a look of disdain before stepping to one side. He was lucky he listened to her otherwise Skylar would have dropped him on his ass. She made her way up to where the woman was sitting in a folding rocking chair.

"Why do you want to see him?"

"I just have a couple more questions."

"Regarding the murder of that man? I heard about that. Terrible thing."

She nodded.

"Ricky! Ricky, get your butt out here." She took a swig of her tea. "He's a good kid. My daughter is too, she just fell in with the wrong man. It was Tucker that got her hooked on drugs."

Bud circled around her and took his seat so he could eavesdrop. He blew out a plume of smoke and rocked back and forth with a deadpan expression.

"You know who supplied her?"

"Do I look like her dealer? Of course not. Me and her had a falling out after she got hitched to that loser." She turned to Bud. "No offense, Bud."

"None taken."

"But my daughter wouldn't be in this mess if it wasn't for him."

"Well I'm sure they will get her in a program for her drug use."

Bud snorted. "That's all you folks do, isn't it? Throw people in prison or put them in a program. Maybe if you actually did some actual detective work, you would find the killer of my brother."

"It's still an open case, Bud. The department has limited resources. They're still looking into it."

"I bet they are," he said, sounding unconvinced.

He took another swig of his beer and sneered. Ricky appeared in the doorway. He was dressed in a Metallica T-shirt and had a ballcap on back to front. His jeans were ripped.

"Yeah?"

"The detective here wants a word with you."

He put down a game controller he was holding and stepped outside. Skylar walked a short distance away to get out of earshot. Ricky looked nervous, he kept adjusting his T-shirt.

"Are you back to bust me for the marijuana?"

She gave a thin smile. "No, but I do need to ask you about it again, and this time I want you to be honest with me." His cheeks became flushed and in that moment, she knew Cole wasn't lying. "You didn't get the bag from Lars Jackson, did you?"

He cleared his throat and shifted from one foot to the next nervously. He looked over at his grandmother and then back at her.

"Come on, Ricky. I know where you got it from, I just

want to hear you tell me."

"He told me to not say anything."

"I know. Now tell me who?"

"Cole Watson." He exhaled and actually looked relieved to have put his name out there.

"He was with you that morning, wasn't he?"

He nodded but didn't elaborate any further.

"Look, I understand you wanting to help someone out but this is serious. A kid just like you lost his father. Now if you could find out who killed your father, wouldn't you want that kid to be honest?"

He shrugged and nodded. "Are you going to lock me away like my mother?"

She stifled a laugh. She always found kids to have a strange view of the police. They were nervous and for good reason. It was good to see a level of respect there as far too often she'd encountered people who had lost it.

"No, but I want you to tell me what happened that morning. Take me through from when you made the arrangement with Lars to heading out there."

"I didn't make the arrangement. Lars swung by our place the night before and spoke to my mom. After he left, she told me that Cole would come by in the morning to pick me up and take me fishing because Lars couldn't."

"So you'd been out with Lars before?"

"Yeah, a couple of times."

"In the same boat?"

"Always."

"Did you hear any of the conversation he had with your mom?"

"A little."

"What time did he arrive?"

"I don't know, maybe sometime after nine. He didn't stay long. Maybe five minutes. He had to rush off, I heard him say something about meeting with a client, something to do with missing money."

"Did he arrive alone?"

Ricky's chin dropped and his eyes darted over to Bud who was studying them.

"Yeah, um..."

Skylar caught the look he threw his uncle, and she motioned with her head for him to walk with her. They began walking down the road that snaked its way around the mobile homes.

"Listen up, Ricky, you're not going to get into trouble but I need you to be honest. Was Cole with Lars that evening?"

He shook his head once they were out of sight of his grandmother and uncle.

"Who was?"

He swallowed hard. "My uncle. Bud. Lars arrived alone but left with my uncle."

Skylar stopped walking. "Are you sure about that?"

"Positive."

She turned to walk back, and he grabbed her by the arm. "You're not going to say anything to him, are you?"

"Not right now."

She caught a look in his eye, one of fear. "Is there anything else you need to tell me, Ricky?"

"No."

"Are you sure?"

He nodded. It couldn't have been easy for the kid being surrounded by people who honestly didn't seem as if they cared about anything else except getting high and drunk. She understood what it was like to grow up around people like that, to live in a state of fear. Her father was always busy working as a cop in New York and trying to talk to him at the end of the day was virtually impossible. By the time he came home she was usually in bed. And on the few occasions she'd tried to tell him about the way her mother was treating her because of alcoholism, he just brushed it off, telling her to not make up stories. She knew now that he had known about her mother's fits of rage and drunken state but chose to ignore it instead. It would have been an embarrassment to him as an officer. Meanwhile, that left Skylar trying to navigate life with an alcoholic mother, a task that wasn't easy, and no doubt contributed to her finding solace in the bottom of a bottle.

After returning Ricky to his grandmother, she placed

another call to Rachel Sampson under the watchful eye of Bud. There was no answer. She hung up and sat in her vehicle for a moment contemplating what to do next. She couldn't take Bud in just because he was with Lars that night, they needed more, something that could pin them together at the time of the murder.

Chapter 19

It was early evening by the time Skylar managed to pull herself away from the department. Davenport had called her into the office because he wanted an update on the case and he was getting mixed information from Hanson and Reznik. Harvey wasn't answering his phone, which only added fuel to the fire. By the time she got out of there, she wasn't slightly annoyed; she was pissed off. There was nothing worse than office politics to slow things down. She rarely had to deal with it when she was in the U.S. Marshals, and it was part of the reason why she'd walked away from being a cop in New York.

When she arrived at Rachel's home the lights were out, but her vehicle was in the driveway, and beside that was a 4x4 Chevy. She gave the door a knock but got no answer. So she tried ringing the bell. A light came on, and when the door cracked open, a tearful Rachel appeared. She held up tissues to her eyes. She opened the door just enough to speak with her.

"Everything okay?" Skylar asked.

Her eyes darted around nervously. "I'm fine. Just tired."

"I was hoping to speak to you about your husband's financial records."

"This is really not a good time. Can you come back in the morning?"

"But this won't take long."

"I'm sorry but I can't do this now."

She closed the door before Skylar could squeeze another word out. That was odd. The light inside turned off, and she walked back to her truck. There was definitely something odd about her behavior. Of course she understood she was upset about losing her husband but her persistence in wanting Skylar to leave, the look in her eyes, she'd seen that before — in the face of abused women, or those fearful for their life.

She glanced at the 4x4 out front and looked at the license plate.

Skylar got back in her vehicle and fired up the engine, she pulled out of the driveway and hung a right and floored it. She got about half a mile from the home when she swerved the vehicle around and headed back. However, this time she brought it into a rest stop and shut off the lights and engine, and called into dispatch and had them run the license plate.

She waited to hear back from Lt. Lucy Wyner in dispatch. There was no movement coming from Rachel's home but her gut told her something wasn't right. She'd shown up at hundreds of doors over the years and had become attuned to telling when people were either lying or were in trouble.

The radio crackled. "Chevy belongs to a Bud Jennings."

Skylar's eyes widened. "Thanks, Lucy. Can you get hold of Harvey and tell him I'm over at Rachel Sampson's home? Also if there is an officer in the area I'm going to need assistance."

Now under any other conditions she might have

waited for more officers to arrive but if Bud was in there with her, it could turn into a hostage and negotiation situation real fast and not only would that jeopardize Rachel's life but it would get the attention of the Jacksons. That was the last thing she wanted. She checked that the magazine in her Glock was loaded before pushing out of the vehicle and running at a crouch across the road and into the tree line.

Under the cover of darkness, Skylar darted out and slipped around the side keeping her weapon low. She moved around the back of the home until she was close to the windows. She could already hear a male voice seeping out an open window. Hugging the wall with her back she cut the corner before sliding along beneath the windows.

"Where is it?"

Through tears Rachel replied, "I don't know. He never mentioned anything like that."

"You're lying. He was about to move. I want that money otherwise you won't see your kid again, and you'll join your husband."

Skylar peeked in the window and saw two figures. One was watching over her while the other was rooting through drawers. Both of them had ski masks on, and one of them was tugging out drawer after drawer.

She moved along under the window heading for the back door.

"I swear, if you don't tell us now, I will——."

Her foot stepped on a branch and it cracked.

"You hear that?"

"Go check it."

"Why me?"

"Because I'm telling you. Now go check it out."

Skylar pulled back behind the corner of the wall just as the storm door on the rear entrance opened. She heard boots against the porch step and then they vanished.

"No one's there."

She could hear the men getting even more annoyed but it was when they struck her that she knew she had to get in. Her backup was not there, but she didn't have time to wait. She hurried towards the back door and carefully squeezed the handle to open it. Storm doors were notorious for making a squeaking noise from the spring on the door. As she eased it open, she had to do it really slow to avoid being heard. Unfortunately luck wasn't on her side. The door creaked, and she knew right then that things were about to go south.

Skylar burst through the rear door with firearm raised.

"Police. Put it down!"

One of them made a dash for the front door while the other lifted a gun. She fired off two rounds dropping him before hurrying in.

"You okay?"

"They've got my kid."

Skylar took off in pursuit of the second intruder. By the time she made it to the front door she heard someone slam a door on the truck outside. The engine roared, and it shot into reverse as she came out. She raised her weapon and fired one round after the next at the front of the engine until the driver veered out and slammed into a tree on the other side of the road. She released the magazine and slapped in a new one as she calmly approached the vehicle.

Whoever was inside was slumped over the wheel.

She got on the radio to find out where her assistance was. Dispatch told her they were on their way. As she opened the door on the vehicle a phone dropped from a hand gloved in blood. Several of her rounds had struck him and he was bleeding out. She tore off the ski mask to find Bud Jennings coughing up blood.

"Too late," he said with a smirk. Her eyes dropped to the ground where his phone was. She reached in and grabbed it up and looked at the caller ID. It was for Lars Jackson's place: Jackson's River Fishing and Sightseeing Tours.

A flash of blue and red lights and a set of headlights washed over the road as a cruiser came barreling down. The siren was wailing as it came to a halt not far from Bud's vehicle.

Deputy Stephens hopped out, his vehicle was closely followed by another which had Reznik inside. As soon as they arrived, Skylar quickly filled Reznik in on what she knew before making a dash back to her truck. She wasn't even a few yards from it when a call came in from Harvey.

"You choose now to phone? Where have you been?"

"Chasing up leads. What's going on? I got a call from Lucy."

"Lars has Rachel's kid. Bud Jennings was holding Rachel hostage demanding that she give them the money."

"I know. The surveillance video at the ATM, and in the stores near the coroner's office came up empty, however, the cameras at a store across from Lars's business picked up two vehicles entering the lot that night. Ted's and Lars's. Bud and Lars got out along with Ted and entered the establishment. Bud came out an hour and a half later and drove Ted's truck away."

She put him on speakerphone as she hopped into her truck and brought it to life. It let out a guttural roar as she gunned the engine and tore away from the hard shoulder.

"But that's not all. The amount Ted pulled from the account on the day he was murdered was…"

"Seven thousand, four hundred," Skylar said cutting him off.

"How did you know?"

"Going by the pattern of wires. That was the amount he was transferring each time. I'm going out on a limb here but I think I know what was going on. Based on the money that was going into the offshore account and coming out of the other account, it looks as if he was skimming off the top."

"Which would explain why he was wanting to get out of town. So where is the money they're after?"

"Still in the offshore account. He must have been the only one who had access to that. I figure it was Lars that had Ted set up the offshore account as all the investors had one."

Silence stretched between them for a few seconds.

Skylar continued, "So William Akitt must have made arrangements with Tito and the Latin Syndicate to act as the supplier of drugs. They would have needed someone to collect and distribute the shipments and there is no one more qualified than Lars Jackson. Lars must have collected, distributed and got the money and then either wired that into the offshore accounts of investors or gave it to them to deposit. William laundered the money by running it through the site. Once it was run through the gambling site, William got his cut and no one would say a thing as it was earned through gambling. William must have assumed he was getting his fair share of the drug money. Lars was then having Ted pay him his portion; except I think Lars was holding back on William and telling him he was making less than he actually was. Ted was the only one in the know about how much was hitting that offshore account. Ted tried to use that to his advantage and was keeping the largest amount of it in the offshore account and was hoping to leave the state before Lars requested it. William must have got wind of what was being made from the distributing of drugs and realized he was getting cut out of the lion's share and so

Lars must have panicked and told him that Ted was stealing from him. So Lars kills Ted and makes it look like he committed suicide. William thinks Ted has the money, and we cops think that Ted killed himself. That way William doesn't come after Lars, and neither do we."

"And Bud Jennings?"

"That's the tricky part. If I'm not mistaken, I would say he was involved in the death of his own brother, Tucker. Why? The day I arrived Laura was servicing him. He wanted her to himself."

"Or maybe he got tired of seeing him beating Laura around."

"Who knows? There will be plenty of time to figure that out but right now we need to get Rachel's kid back. I'm heading for…"

"Jackson's River Fishing and Sightseeing Tours," Harvey said cutting her off. "I'm already halfway there."

Chapter 20

Lies. Everyone told them. Sometimes it was to protect others, but more often than not, it was to protect oneself. Except now it wasn't for her, it was to protect Harvey. He had a family to think about and after seeing his hesitation in the high-speed pursuit; she wasn't going to put him in this position. Not after all he'd been through with the Jacksons and the loss of his sister.

She swerved the vehicle and headed in the direction of Royal City.

Skylar figured Lars wouldn't have been stupid enough to kidnap the boy unless he was under extreme pressure from William Akitt to come up with his money. He certainly wouldn't have kept the boy at his place of work. It was too risky, and besides, Callum owned it.

It didn't take her more than fifteen minutes to arrive. The streets were quiet as she stepped out of her truck in the empty lot outside the company. She collected two more magazines and made her way around to the back where the warehouse was. She made it to the corner and saw several trucks, one of which was an F150 with the logo of Jackson's River Fishing and Sightseeing Tours on the outside. Bingo, she thought.

"This is your fault," she heard William's voice. "Take the kid and get rid of him. The rest of you, shut this place down. We are getting out tonight."

"And we were just getting to know each other," Skylar said slipping through a doorway into the back of the warehouse. The sound of guns cocking brought everyone to attention. William turned. He had four other men with him, two of whom looked to be part of the Latin Syndicate. Meanwhile Lars Jackson was holding a gun to the kid's head.

Skylar kept her Glock trained on William. "Tell me, William, are you a gambling man?"

William locked his eyes on her as she moved in closer. "How about you tell your men to put their weapons down?"

He stared at her, not saying anything. Skylar motioned to Jaden, and he took a step towards her but was quickly yanked back by Lars.

"Really?" Skylar said. "We're going to do it this way? Look, it's over, we know you've been using Royal City as a front for laundering drug money, and I know that Lars here was screwing you over."

William diverted his gaze to Lars who was shaking his head.

"Oh," Skylar laughed. "Was I not meant to say that? My bad!"

"Lars?"

"I don't know what she's on about."

"Dear me, do I have to explain everything? Your buddy here was giving you seventy-five percent of what he was taking in. The other twenty-five percent he was keeping for himself and using Ted Sampson in the process. Except Ted wised up, didn't he, Lars? He figured he would hold back on you like you were holding back on William. He was going to do a run to Colorado but before that, William figured out that you were cutting him out of the full profits and he demanded the money. But you weren't going to pay it so you told him Ted had taken it. Now I figure you told William here you would get it but instead you offed him to make it look like it was a suicide because you couldn't have him telling William what was going on. But William here still wanted his money, so you thought Ted's wife might give you either the money or the card to access the offshore account, except you screwed up the supposed suicide. But that's neither here nor there. Now let the kid go, and we can all go and have a nice little chat that will clear this all up."

A gun fired, and a bullet grazed Skylar's leg.

As she hit the floor, chaos erupted as she returned fire and scrambled for cover.

Her heart was hammering in her chest as she pressed her back against one of the shelving units. Every few seconds she'd look down the aisle and see one or two of William's men fanning out. Outside she heard the sound of a truck, and she darted to the door under the hail of gunfire and burst outside in time to see Lars pulling away without the boy.

His truck hadn't made it around the corner when another vehicle struck it from the side. *That's mine.* The collision was hard and slammed Lars's truck into a black sedan, sandwiching it.

"What the heck?"

In the front seat was Harvey. *Impossible, he should have been across town.*

She didn't have time to question it any further as more rounds echoed overhead.

Skylar turned and squeezed off several rounds taking down one of William's men.

She took cover behind a line of shelves and continued to keep them under fire even at the sound of sirens in the distance. Beyond the windows blue and red lit up the night as multiple cruisers came in cutting off whatever means of escape William had in mind.

"All right. Don't shoot!" Gingerly he came out into the aisle with his hands up, as did three of his men, the fourth remained lifeless nearby.

As officers from the Carrabelle Police Department and deputies from Franklin County swarmed the warehouse, Skylar discovered Jaden huddled in a corner.

"It's okay, Jaden," she said. "It's all over. Give me your hand."

She reached for his and he clasped hers and clung to her.

Skylar staggered, her leg in pain, her jeans covered in blood.

Harvey was in the middle of talking to some of the Carrabelle police when she emerged with Jaden. He broke away and walked over, his eyes narrowing.

"Does it hurt?" he asked as she handed off the boy to an officer who led him away to be reunited with his mother.

"Like hell."

She hobbled out of the warehouse heading towards her truck, or what was left of it.

"Good. Maybe next time you won't exclude me."

"Oh come on, Harv."

Harvey motioned to a medic to come over to tend to her.

"How did you know?"

"You might have been a U.S. Marshal, but I've been at this longer than you, Reid."

"So you figured I had your best interest at heart and was leading you away from danger?"

"No, I just know the Jacksons like the back of my hand and he would have never brought the kid to Callum's place of business."

She smiled. "Great minds do think alike."

"I don't know if I like my mind being compared to yours," Harvey said.

She reached her truck and took in the sight of the front end which was absolutely destroyed. "Oh man, really? My truck?"

"Now we're even," he said walking away with a smile on his face.

She got this confused expression on her face. "But I

don't get it. How did you—?"

"You left the keys inside, and I certainly wasn't going to barrel in here with my rental. I figured if we had to chase someone else down, at least this time it would be yours that got wrecked." He grinned as a medic came over and tried to convince her to lay down so he could take a look.

"It's just a graze."

Blue and red lights strobed the sky as William, his men and a battered-looking Lars were read their Miranda rights and taken into custody.

***

Ten days later, after taking some time off to heal and recover, Skylar had just got off the phone with Scot who was making arrangements to come down and see her in a month, when she heard Harvey's voice outside.

"Permission to come aboard."

"Permission not granted," she yelled with a smile. She heard his boots land on the deck and the boat shifted a little. Skylar got up and tried to clear up the mess. Trash cans were overflowing and paperwork and a week's worth of takeout food boxes were still on the table. The doors opened, and he stepped down into the salon.

"Holy cow. You ever thought about hiring a maid?"

"Looks are deceiving, aren't they?"

"Sure are. I finally get around to seeing your boat and I think you've hit the jackpot with this catamaran and then I step down into hell itself."

His eyes washed over the disorder. Harvey was holding in his hand a bag.

"What you got there?"

"I thought I would bring you some lunch."

"It's from Barb, isn't it?"

He paused for a second, then grinned. "Yeah."

Harvey put the bag down and reached in and started bringing out different foiled containers of food. "She's determined to win you over."

"Well, between her and Donnie, I'm staying well fed and thoroughly caffeinated."

She pointed to some of the food boxes and empty cups

that had the Vagabond logo on the side. Harvey took a seat and put his arms back. "Man, this is comfortable. I could get used to this. How's your leg?"

She nodded. "Better. I should be back in on Monday."

He rolled his eyes. "And just when I was getting used to peace and quiet," he joked.

"So how did it go?"

"Not good for the Jacksons. Callum showed up the day we brought Lars in but even with his money and lawyers he couldn't do squat. Bud pulled through and confessed to get a lesser sentence. He said that he was involved in the disposal of Ted's body, along with his brother's, but he also revealed an interesting tidbit that we didn't know." He cleared his throat. "It seems that the reason Ted marked Tucker's death as inconclusive was so he could use it as ammo against Lars."

"You mean Lars knew that he was holding back money?"

"Seems so. According to Bud's statement, Lars killed Tucker because of the way he was treating Laura. He had a thing for her, but so did Bud, that's why he agreed to dispose of the body. Ted did the autopsy and realized that he'd been murdered but by that point he was already deep in Lars's pocket laundering money. He marked the death as inconclusive and then decided to flip the tables and told Lars he wanted more of a cut. I guess Lars didn't take too kindly to that and after William found out from one of his suppliers that they were being undercut — the rest is history. Lars strangled Ted that night out at his place of business and took his body in one of his vehicles when he took the boat out there that night for Ricky the next morning. Bud was already out there in the vehicle waiting for him. They tried to make it look like a suicide in the hope that William would back off. He didn't, so they knew they needed to get their hands on that money, so they kidnapped the kid thinking Ted had withdrawn the money from the offshore account or still had access to it."

Skylar nodded.

"But Bud would have had to step into the soil to get to the boat, right? And there was only one set of footprints found and that was Cole's."

"Not exactly. The driver's side was pulled up close to thick woodland. It was the passenger side that was facing the muddy area. He must have clambered over branches and kept himself off the ground. I mean, based on the number of broken branches that's what the crime team have surmised."

"Well I'll be damned," Skylar said.

Harvey took in his surroundings as he handed her some lunch. "I really think you should get a real place. I can't imagine living here can be good for your sanity."

"I beg to differ. The lapping of waves. The sound of gulls. The smell of the coast. It actually is starting to feel like home."

"Really?" He took a bite of his food.

"Why are you surprised?"

"Ah, I just took you for a city girl."

"Things change."

"Does that mean you are going to stay with the department?"

"For now."

He wiped the corner of his mouth. "So you like Florida?"

She shrugged. "It's growing on me."

She smiled and both of them began tucking into Barb's fish sandwiches and conch fritters.

* * *

THANK YOU FOR READING

Please take a second to leave a review, even if it's only 10 words. It's much appreciated.

A Plea

Thank you for reading DEAD CALM. If you enjoyed the book, I would really appreciate it if you would consider leaving a review. Without reviews, an author's books are virtually invisible on the retail sites. It also lets me know what you liked. You can leave a review by visiting the book's page. I would greatly appreciate it. It only takes a couple of seconds.

Thank you — **Emma Rose Watts**

Newsletter

Thank you for buying Dead Calm: Coastal Suspense Series Book 1 published by Coastal Publishing.

Click here to receive special offers, bonus content, and news about new Emma Rose Watts books. Sign up for the newsletter. http://www.emmarosewatts.com/

About the Author

Emma Rose Watts is the not so cozy pen name of the bestselling cozy mystery author Emma Watts. Under the name Emma Rose Watts, she writes gritty suspense and mysteries based in Florida. She is from Maine. She is married, and has kids and a dog.

Made in the USA
Columbia, SC
09 December 2020